A Gem Of

A Murder

Nanci M. Pattenden

A Gem of a Murder

Copyright © 2025 Nanci M. Pattenden

This is a work of fiction. All characters, names, incidents, organizations, and dialogue in this novel are either the products of the author's imagination or are used fictitiously.

Published by Murder Does Pay, Ink
Ontario, Canada
www.murderdoespayink.ca

The views expressed in this work are solely those of the author and do not necessarily reflect the views of the publisher, and the publisher hereby disclaims any responsibility for them.

ISBN: 978-1-998860-11-1
e-ISBN: 978-1-998860-12-8

1 2 3 4 5 6 7 8 9 0

Detective Hodgins Victorian Murder Mysteries

Body in the Harbour

Death on Duchess Street

Corpses for Christmas

Books 1 to 3 Collection

Homicide on the Homestead

United in Holy Deadlock

Abduction of Life

Books 4 to 6 Collection

Generation Witch

Rebirth

Awakening

D.E.M.ON. Tales Series

Assassin Eco-Corpses

Bobcat Got Your Tongue?

A Craptacular Understatement

Double Dog Dare Ya

Even Equines Don't Like Liver

Frozen Foes & Dominos

Growing Up Grim

Hoodoo In The Loo

The Improbable Goog Pursuit

Junk In The Trunk

Kids Can Be Such A Pain

ACKNOWLEDGMENTS

I'd like to say a great big thanks to Brew It Coffee Bar in Newmarket for providing a wonderful environment in which to work. The coffee is constantly flowing and the treats are yummy.

As always, thanks to my editor, MJ Moores of Infinite Pathways, and Christopher Watts, my graphics guru.

THANK YOU

CHAPTER ONE

Constable John Duggan of the Toronto Constabulary yawned, making his way through the warehouses along the shore of Lake Ontario, lantern held high in front of him, checking each padlock, confirming they were secure. As he approached the last building, scuffling and nearby voices caught his attention.

"I don't have the money. Not all of it. Here. Take this. Two hundred and thirty-seven dollars. I need time to get the rest."

"Ain't good enough. Boss says he wants the entire lot, plus the merchandise. A thousand, plus another five bills interest. If ya ain't got it, my friend here is gonna have ta make an example of ya."

The constable tried to follow the voices, but they stopped as quickly as they began. "Hello? Is someone there? Do you need assistance?"

A thud sounded, then more scuffling from behind a building closer to the train tracks than the shore. When he made his way to where he thought the voices came from, he found no one. Only a brown felt derby hat, partially crushed, lay upside down by the rail tracks. A scruffy cat squeezed through a broken board on a small tool shed, one ear half gone.

"Hmm. Must have scarpered off. Did you see where they went, puss?"

The cat slunk away, and the constable resumed his rounds.

* * *

Four hours later, Mrs. Burtchall made her way to work at Gooderham and Worts Distillery. As charlady, she had to make certain her boss's office was clean, all the wastebaskets emptied, and the desks dust-free before he arrived. As she approached the side door, she spotted several barrels stacked along the outer wall. Something lay draped over one. She stopped and lifted it off.

"Perfectly good sack coat. Who'd a throwed that out?" She held it in front of her. "That might fit my Jack." As she turned the coat to examine it, something dripped on her boot. "Why's it wet? Ain't rained in days."

She looked down. The ground around the barrel had several dark patches leaching outward. Thinking the barrel may still hold whisky, she reached for the lid, setting it on top of the one beside it. Mrs. Burtchall took one look inside, dropped the coat, and ran looking for the closest constable, work all but forgotten.

* * *

Mrs. Burtchall stopped running at Derby Street, holding her side while trying to catch her breath. "Behind Gooderham and Worts Distillery." She pointed south. "Cut across the laneway off Parliament Street, north side of the building, just before you get to Esplanade. At the side entrance." She paused and took a deep breath. "Spotted a sack coat and thought my Jack could use it. Jack's me husband. Anyway, that's when I noticed somethin' funny. Ground were wet. Thought some lout put out a barrel with whisky still in it. Opened the barrel, and that's when I saw him. Seen a few dead men in my time, so I knew there weren't no hurry. Only ran 'cuz I'm gonna be late for work." She stopped to take another breath. "Hoped to find a constable on the way, but didn't see a one till now."

Duggan took down everything thing she said. "We'll look into it right away. I heard a scuffle on the docks not far from Gooderham's several hours ago. Wonder if this chap was involved? My shift's almost over. Why don't you come to the station with me and I'll see if one of the detectives is in yet."

Duggan and Burtchall rushed up Parliament to Wilton, both breathless after hurrying to Station Number Four.

Duggan spotted Constable Barnes hanging up his coat and called out. "Henry, can you take care of Mrs. Burtchall? Seems she's found a dead man. My shift's over, but I'll stop at the coroner's and leave word for Dr. Stonehouse. Here. Take my notebook. Just leave it on my desk and I'll get it tomorrow." He handed the book to Barnes and made a hasty exit.

"I gotta get to work. Boss ain't tolerant of tardiness, and I need my pay." Mrs. Burtchall backed away from Barnes' desk.

"This will only take a minute." Barnes glanced at Duggan's scribbling. "You found him in a whisky barrel? Fill me in on the way. Just have to leave a note for Detective Hodgins, then I'll flag down a hansom."

"A ride?" She released a soft sigh. "Maybe I won't git docked too much pay."

Five minutes passed before any type of buggy came by. They clambered in, anxious to arrive at the distillery before too many workers trampled through the crime scene. With most businesses still not open for the day, the horse made record time getting down to the harbour. The sack coat lay on the ground where Burtchall, the charlady, left it. The barrel still sat open, a slight aroma of whisky wafting out.

"Tell me what you touched before you go inside. Are you sure you're feeling up to work?"

"Course I am. Not letting no dead man deprive me of a day's wages. Gonna get docked as it is."

Barnes took down her home address before she slipped through the side door, then examined the area while waiting for Detective Hodgins and Doctor Stonehouse. By the time the clomping of the horse and buggy alerted him to the arrival of the coroner, Barnes had completed a detailed sketch of the laneway.

"Mornin' Doc. Not the best way to start the day."

"Morning. At least we've started better than this poor chap. Is the detective on his way?" The doctor hopped off his wagon and joined the constable by the side door.

"Left him a note. Don't know if he's in yet or not. Say, how are you and the Missus coping with the baby?"

"He's a joy, and not exactly a baby anymore. Over a year old now."

Barnes smiled. "That's good to hear. How are the twins with him, if you don't mind me asking? I know they've met."

Stonehouse leaned against the building. "Don't mind at all. You already know he's their baby brother. They're all too young to be told they're adopted and siblings, but by the time they're told, they'll be fast friends."

"Amazing how you and the detective adopted the children of a murderess." Barnes sighed. "Hopefully, Violet and myself will be blessed soon." After realizing what he said, he grinned and quickly amended. "Blessed with our own children, not that of a murderess."

Stonehouse chuckled. "If not, I highly recommend adoption. Now, shall we get that poor chap out of the barrel and into my wagon?"

"Well, the detective does like to see everything before the body is moved, but we can't check anything, what with him stuffed in there. Wish Riddell was in before I left. He could take a photograph. Didn't have time to grab the camera myself as the lady who found him was headed to the front door." Barnes looked down the lane. "No telling when he'll arrive, so I guess we'd better get this poor chap out so you can examine him."

They agreed the only way to remove the corpse was to destroy the barrel. The man had been jammed in tight. Together, the constable and doctor tipped the cask over, smashing some of the wooden staves and spilling out the remnants of whisky mixed with blood. Once the remaining staves were slipped out of the hoops, the body rolled out.

"He's beginning to stiffen, so my guess is he's been dead somewhere between three to eight hours. And before you ask how I arrived at that, he's not very warm despite the hot weather, so more than three hours, but he's not totally stiff, so less than eight. Now, help me get him into the back of the wagon."

"Where are you taking my body?" Detective Hodgins walked over just as Barnes jumped into the wagon bed, causing him to drop the deceased's legs. "Any idea who he is?"

Barnes grabbed the legs and finished helping Stonehouse load the body. "Not yet, sir. We only just busted him outta the barrel." Barnes pointed at the heap of staves and hoops. "I sketched everything while I waited for the doctor." He handed Hodgins his notebook. "Charlady found a coat and noticed something dripping from it and around the barrel."

"Very good. You're quite the artist, Henry. Where's the coat? Does it belong to the dead man?"

"On the ground where Mrs. Burtchall dropped it. It's half soaked in blood, so I suppose it must belong to him. Doesn't smell like much whisky got absorbed. The barrels are supposed to be empty. Just dribbles left."

"Check the pockets. See if there's anything to identify him. May have been a robbery gone wrong, but why not just leave him on the ground?" The detective pulled at his handlebar moustache.

Barnes checked the coat, holding it away from his body, trying to avoid covering himself with blood. One droplet landed on his shoe with a splat.

Doctor Stonehouse looked in the man's trouser pockets, not as concerned about getting bloody. "No money or pocket watch. Not even a wedding ring." Stonehouse glanced at the coat. "Blood's not dry yet, so this didn't happen all that long ago." He sniffed the coat. "Like Barnes said, slight hint of whisky. Mostly blood keeping it wet. Why did he have a coat in this weather? Suit jacket is quite hot without adding an extra layer."

"Nothing in the coat pockets either, except a hanky." Barnes fished a second book from his pocket. "Duggan left me his notebook. Says shortly after midnight he heard some men arguing near the warehouses just west of here. Found a derby hat on the pier where he thought the voices came from. Reckon it's still there."

Hodgins gave Barnes' notebook back and took Duggan's in exchange. "I wonder, could the constable have interrupted something, and they moved over here to conclude their business? Don't suppose that hanky is monogrammed?"

"No, just plain."

Hodgins shook his head. "Doesn't exactly narrow it down. The cut of the suit indicates the man wasn't destitute, but certainly not expensive enough to be part of the gentry." He turned to the doctor. "Anything you can tell me based on what you see right now?"

"Someone slit his throat. Two deep gashes severed his jugular. More on his neck. I'll give you an exact count after I get him on the table, stripped, and washed. And I guess you noticed the black eye."

The detective nodded. "Yes. The question is, did he receive it in a struggle with his attacker, or is it a result of a totally separate incident?"

"Can tell you that right now. See how it's a deep violet? It wouldn't have occurred too long ago."

"Sir? Maybe he got slugged when Duggan heard the scuffle. He noted a thud. Might have fallen and hit his head, knocking him out. Then they carried him here to finish him off." Barnes looked at Stonehouse. "Is that possible?"

"Anything's possible, constable. I'd like to fully examine him before I speculate. If he has a bump on the back of his head, then yes, he may have fallen when hit. Now, the sooner I get back to my office, the sooner you'll have my report. Detective?"

"Yes, yes. Go ahead. I'll stop in when we've finished here. With luck, you'll find something hidden on him to help with identification." Hodgins gestured at Barnes. "The coat?"

Henry dropped the bloody coat in the doctor's wagon. It landed with a plop, droplets landing on Stonehouse's trousers. "Sorry."

Stonehouse shrugged. "Hazard of the job." He hopped out of the wagon bed and stepped onto the wheel, using the toe board to pull himself up to the seat. The doctor snapped the reins. The horse jerked the buggy forward, leaving the two officers in the laneway.

CHAPTER TWO

Hodgins held his hand out. "Let's have another look at that sketch you drew."

Barnes flipped to the drawing in his notebook before handing it over.

The detective looked from the page to the alley, taking in every detail, mumbling as he walked around the area. "This is as good as a photograph. Better, actually. You paced out distances using your feet as a ruler." Hodgins smiled. "When we get back, we'll measure those oversized dew-beaters of yours and come up with more accurate distances."

Barnes looked down. "You make it sound like I have big feet." He lifted one foot up. "Average size, I'd say."

"Put your foot down before you topple over, and see if that door is unlocked. I'd like to speak with the woman who found him."

"Mrs. Burtchall. Funny thing. She didn't seem at all fazed at finding a dead body."

"Not everyone's as squeamish as you, Henry."

Barnes opened the door and stepped in, inhaling the warm, malty aroma of mashed and fermented barley.

"Can you imagine having to smell this all day? Almost puts me off whisky altogether." The constable wrinkled his nose as he caught a whiff of the slightly sour, tangy smell of yeast.

"Try not to think about it. We need to find Burtchall."

After asking several workers, they were directed to another section of the building containing the office. They found the char cleaning there. She stopped when she noticed Barnes.

"Tol' ya all I know. Got work ta do."

"Please, Mrs. Burtchall, just a moment of your time. I'm Detective Hodgins. I'd like to hear from you exactly what happened. What made you stop and look inside the barrel?"

She sighed. "It's like I tol' the other copper. Spotted a coat and thought it might fit my Jack. Didn't notice the blood right off. Thought it were just wet. Noticed it were damp around the one barrel and figured some fool put out a full barrel by mistake, so I opened it. Ran for a copper when I seed him staring up at me." She looked at Hodgins, one eyebrow raised in hope. "Don't suppose I kin have the coat?"

"Afraid not. You didn't recognize the man? Employee maybe?"

"Didn't get a good look at 'im. Jest dropped the lid and ran. You'll have to check with the foreman to see if anyone's missing. Boss kin give ya the names." She pointed at a closed door. "Mr. Gooderham's in there. Mr. Worts is out on business.

"Thank you, ma'am." Hodgins walked to the door and knocked.

"Come in."

Hodgins opened the door and entered, followed by Barnes. The detective introduced himself and the constable, then explained the reason for the visit.

Gooderham looked shocked. "In one of my barrels? Absurd."

"He was found this morning by your own charwoman. The barrel sat beside the door to one of your buildings. We need to find out if he's an employee."

"I understand. It'll take a while as I have several buildings and many employees. I'll find someone to go around and check, then report back. Where can I find you?"

"Station House Four, on Wilton. If you can find out today, I'd appreciate it. I'd like to inform his family as soon as possible. If you could check to see if anyone noticed someone hanging around close to midnight, that would be helpful. Night watchman, possibly?" Hodgins held up a hand as Gooderham started to protest. "I realize that's an enormous ask considering how many employees you have. A sign posted in each building, perhaps?"

"Yes. I can see to that. My clerk can take care of it. He's delivering something to one of the buildings, but I'll tell him when he returns." He ran a hand over his face. "A body found in one of my barrels. That's not good for business."

"Not good for the deceased, either." Hodgins held out his hand. "Thank you for your time and cooperation."

When they exited, Barnes turned north, back towards the police station. Hodgins turned south.

"This way, Barnes. The sun's higher and should shed more light in the alley. I want to check the entire area, just in case the killer left something behind."

They spent over thirty minutes checking behind every crate and barrel sitting along the side of the building. The only items found were pages of newspapers and a half-eaten piece of bread.

"I think we've given this as good a look-over as we can. Which dock or wharf did Duggan hear the argument?"

"Let me check." Barnes was about to drop the newspaper he'd picked up, stopping as something caught his eye. "Sir, look." He joined the detective on the opposite side of the lane and handed him the paper.

"Interesting. Could be something or nothing. Many people read papers from New York, especially business owners."

"The *Times*, yes. But how popular is The *Brooklyn Daily Eagle*? Can't be many newsstands that carry it."

"You've got a point." Hodgins folded it and put it in his jacket pocket. "The argument on the wharf?"

Barnes flipped through to the last of Duggan's notes. "Looks like it was the one right below Gooderham's."

"Right. Let's have a look down there. Maybe by the time we've finished, Stonehouse will at least be able to tell us if he's found any identification on the man."

CHAPTER THREE

Finding nothing except the hat Duggan noted, Hodgins sent Barnes back to the station while he stopped at the morgue.

"Give me a few more hours, detective. I've barely begun." Stonehouse dried his hands and tossed the towel onto an empty examination table.

"Not looking for your findings. Have you gone through his clothing?" Hodgins glanced at the half-covered body on the steel table.

"No. Wanted to get him washed and examined first. Only just finished cleaning him." The coroner pointed to the table beside the corpse where the clothing had been piled. "By all means, help yourself. You can find a pair of gloves in the cabinet, unless you want to get covered in blood. Might want to put on an apron, too. He soaked in his blood for several hours. When you're finished with them, they'll go in an incinerator once they've dried."

Hodgins mumbled a thank you and donned a spare apron hanging on a peg, then rooted through the cabinets for gloves. He walked over to the table and stared at the clothing. "Where to start?"

"There's no good place." Stonehouse turned around to face him. "It's all a mess. Just start at the top and work your way down, or vice versa. That's what I generally do."

"Hmm. We've already had a look in the pockets of his overcoat. Just don't understand why he wore one in this heat. Suppose I should check the lining to see if anything's been hidden."

The detective laid the coat out and ran his fingers around the sleeve cuffs, feeling for any lumps and bumps. Nothing seemed amiss, so he moved to the bottom seam. Again, nothing. Next, he checked the left seam, then the right. He examined the stitching on either side of the front opening and around the buttonholes. Ready to give up, he discovered something hard around the bottom buttonhole.

"Doctor, have you a pair of scissors?"

"Found something? Should be a pair on my desk." Stonehouse stopped his post-mortem and watched as the detective grabbed the scissors and snipped at the threads.

Once cut, Hodgins used his thumb and index finger to squeeze the object through the tiny opening.

Both men whistled.

The detective held the object up. "So, is this man a smuggler or a jewel thief?"

Stonehouse wiped his hands and clapped Hodgins on the back. "Always thinking the best of people. How do you know the chap isn't the owner of the ruby and was trying to hide it from a thief?"

Hodgins laughed. "Hazard of the trade. I suppose after all these years I expect shady business when people hide things. Haven't had time to read the paper lately, and no reports have crossed my desk. Have you read of any jewel thefts recently?"

"No. Nothing around the city, at least."

"The city? Almost forgot." Hodgin removed the folded newspaper page from his jacket pocket. "Barnes found this near the body. A torn page from the *Brooklyn Daily Eagle*. I'll make enquires when I get back to the station."

Hodgins set the tiny gem aside and continued searching the victim's clothing while Stonehouse got on with the autopsy.

Finding nothing more in the sack coat, Hodgins rechecked the trouser pockets before going through the seams. Both cuffs hid numerous small rubies and emeralds.

"I'll need to borrow a small lidded jar or vial, doctor." Hodgins opened the cuff seam further, careful not to let the contents fall out.

"My hands are covered in blood. Amazing how much he still had in his veins. Help yourself. Cupboard over my desk." Stonehouse half turned. "More rubies?"

"Yes, and emeralds. Small ones." Hodgins opened the cupboard and selected a four-inch cobalt blue bottle with a glass stopper, giving it a quick shake. "Has this bottle been used?"

"No. Everything in that cupboard is new."

"Good. The poison bottle should keep people away from it. Most everyone knows blue is deadly." Hodgins set it beside the trousers and dropped all the tiny coloured gems into it, then reached for the jar of cotton balls, stuffing enough in the little bottle to prevent rattling. He went back to searching the remaining pieces of clothing, finding nothing more.

"Looks like that's all for the clothes. Only thing left is his shoes."

Hodgins reached inside and felt something bunched into the toe of the left shoe. He removed a piece of paper and spread it flat. "Found an address and something written in a foreign language."

"Let me see." The doctor wiped his hands on a mostly clean towel and took the paper. "Dutch. *Kom, Kom met haast.* It means come, come in haste."

"You're full of surprises, doctor."

"Grew up next door to a Dutch family. We taught each other. This phrase was easy. It almost sounds the same in English. Should have my report ready in a couple more hours."

* * *

When the detective returned to Station House Four, Barnes sat at his desk with the Toronto Directory, making a list.

"Look this up for me, Henry." He handed him the paper from the shoe. Hodgins glanced at the constable's notes. "What are you searching for?"

"Newsstands. Thought I'd go around and see who carries that Brooklyn newspaper. What's this address?"

"That's what you're going to tell me. It was stuffed in the dead man's shoe." He reached into his pocket and placed the blue bottle on Barne's desk.

"Poison? Was that in his shoe, too?"

"Open it."

Barnes raised an eyebrow, then shook the bottle. "Empty?"

"Only of poison. Look inside."

The constable removed the stopper and cotton, holding the bottle steady.

"Tip it into your hand, slowly." Hodgins watched as Barnes' eyes widened.

"My word! Is the dead man a jeweller?"

"I've never heard of a jeweller sewing his wares into his seams. Put them back then continue looking for newsagents. After you look up that address."

"Right away." Barnes slipped the gems back into the bottle then checked the address on the crumpled paper. "It's a boarding house. What about those words? How will you translate it?"

"It seems the good doctor speaks Dutch. Sound it out. Apparently, it's an easy translation."

"*Kom, kom.* Sounds like come. *Met haast.* Haste? Come in haste?"

"Very good. You've got your assignment." Hodgins pointed at the list Barnes complied. "Finish that. I need to send Riddell out. Where is he?"

"We sent him for tea. Almost out."

"Glad he's being put to good use." Hodgins chuckled. "When he returns, tell him to take the equipment to the morgue and photograph the victim. Just his face. Stonehouse has him cleaned up. Is he able to handle everything himself? It's a lot to both carry the equipment and handle his cane."

Barnes waved a hand. "Not a problem. He has a solution. His mother sewed a large sack for the tripod and attached a rope at the top and bottom. Just has to sling the rope over his shoulder, leaving him a free hand for the camera."

"Good. Once I have the photograph, I'll visit the boarding house to find out who our mystery man is. Meanwhile, I have a telegram to send to New York.

CHAPTER FOUR

After much deliberation, the detective decided to send a telegram to Captain Thomas Harrison, the police officer who came up from New York when young Olivia had been murdered in her home a few years earlier. Although they didn't agree on how suspects should be handled, he had been of some help.

Hodgins just couldn't shake the image of a beaten Calhoon, slumped against the wall, Harrison ready to punch him again. The message was brief, a simple inquiry about any recent jewel thefts of rubies and emeralds. He hoped Harrison didn't hold a grudge.

After carefully wording the telegram and giving it to Cooper to send, Hodgins waited for Riddell. The young constable returned from his errand less than five minutes after Hodgins got comfortable behind his desk.

"Tom." Hodgins waved him in. "Grab the camera. I need you to go to the morgue and photograph a face. A body was found earlier this morning, and he has no identification." He came around the desk. "Here, give me the tea. I'll put it away while you gather what you need.

Think I'll come with you to see if Stonehouse has any more information."

Twenty minutes later, Riddell set up the tripod and camera beside the autopsy table, the deceased still covered by a white sheet.

"I'm ready, doctor. Can I uncover his head?"

"Yes. He's been cleaned up. Fortunately, the only injury to his face is the black eye."

Riddell lowered the sheet a little too far, exposing the slashed throat. "Heavens to Betsy! Someone certainly didn't like this fellow."

Stonehouse glanced over. "If you intend on showing that picture around, may I suggest you tuck the sheet under his chin?"

The constable reached for the sheet, then paused.

"The man's dead, Tom. He won't bite you." Hodgins walked over to pull the sheet up to cover the marks on the victim's neck. "Good Lord! Hardly anything left of his neck." He tucked the sheet under as best he could. "Take a few. If you can stomach it, get the wounds, too. Only for the file. The public doesn't need to see those." Hodgins joined the doctor.

"Not a pretty sight, is it?" Stonehouse sat on the edge of his desk. "Haven't begun to write up the report for you yet. The only wounds are on his neck and eye. Bump on the back of his head. He has two deep gashes that severed his jugular. In total, I counted eighteen stab wounds, in addition to the slit throat. He has twelve stabs on the left side of his neck and six on the right. Right ones are deeper and made by a different knife. Smaller."

Hodgins raised an eyebrow. "Two assailants? Interesting."

Metal crashed. The detective and the doctor turned.

"Tom!" Hodgins raced to the constable, who lay unconscious on the floor.

Stonehouse joined him and together they got him onto an empty examination table. A tray of medical instruments lay scattered on the floor. The doctor waved smelling salts under Riddell's nose.

Riddell took a deep breath, then opened his eyes. When he attempted to get up, the doctor stopped him.

"Lay still a moment and take several deep breaths." Satisfied he was all right, Stonehouse let Riddell sit on the edge of the table. "You've a gash on your forehead. Let me clean it. You'll need a stitch or two."

The doctor retrieved what he needed and applied antiseptic to the wound. Riddell winced.

"Sorry. Not used to working on living patients. This will hurt a little." Stonehouse put two stitches in to close up the gash.

Riddell closed his eyes, grimacing. "Good thing your patients are all dead. That hurt more than a little."

"What happened?" Hodgins didn't know whether he should laugh or be concerned. The corner of his mouth twitched as he repressed a chuckle. "I think Barnes is rubbing off on you."

"Sorry, sir, Doctor. It's just… all those wounds. How is his head still attached?"

"Don't worry." Hodgins placed a hand on Riddell's shoulder. "It is a pretty gruesome sight. Did you manage to get enough photographs?"

"Yes, I believe so. Is the equipment damaged?"

"It's fine. You fell away from it and hit the table you're sitting on."

The constable looked down, immediately hopping off. "Is this an autopsy table?"

Stonehouse chuckled. "It's clean. Scrub them down after every use, and this one hasn't been used for days. Now, if there isn't anything else, I'll pick up my instruments, clean them, then start on the report."

* * *

When they arrived back at the police station, Hodgins called out to Barnes. "Would you mind developing the photos? Riddell hit his head and shouldn't be standing around the chemicals. Doctor wants him sitting as much as possible the rest of the day."

"My word! What happened to you?" Barnes stared at Riddell's stitched forehead as he took the camera and plates. "Imagine that's what Frankenstein's monster looked like."

"Let him rest, Henry. I need the prints now."

"Yes, sir." Henry hurried to the back to develop the pictures in the makeshift lab set up in an old storage closet.

When Barnes had the prints ready, Hodgins took the photo of the victim's face and left the others on his desk.

"Barnes, have you had a chance to look for the seller of the Brooklyn newspaper?"

"No. Was just getting ready to start talking to them when you came in."

"Get going, then." Hodgins waved the photograph. "I'm going to show this at the boarding house address written on the paper hidden in the shoe."

CHAPTER FIVE

The detective made his way to 158 King Street West. The front door stood open, allowing the breeze to blow through. Hodgins poked his head in and called out. "Mr. Thompson? Police. I'd like a word."

A man's voice came from one of the rooms. "Be with you in a minute."

Hodgins stepped inside uninvited, and took in the surroundings. Though better than most boarding houses in the city, it wasn't among the best. The wallpaper in the hall peeled a bit, and the rug looked like it could use a good beating.

"What's he done now?"

Hodgins turned. A middle-aged man walked out of the room to the left of the front door. His jacket hung on his gaunt frame, trousers sagging.

"You don't look surprised to see me. Who do you think I'm here about?" Hodgins removed his notebook and pencil from his jacket pocket.

Thompson looked the detective over. "Police, you said. You're not the regular constable."

"Detective Hodgins. You having trouble with one of your boarders?"

The landlord nodded. "Yes. Old Mr. Grant. He's harmless, just a little, um, free, shall we say? With other people's things. Mostly other boarders. They let me know if something's missing, and I search his room when he leaves."

"I see. No one presses charges?"

"Once, when he took a piece of fruit from a grocer. I paid for the apple, and the grocer let it go. Never needed to have a detective come."

"The man I'm here about is in his thirties. Not likely to be called old man." Hodgins took the photograph from another pocket. "Does this man reside here?"

Thompson took the picture. "Yes. Only been here 'bout a week. What's he done to need a detective looking for him?"

"Unfortunately, he died, and we don't know his identity. This address was on a piece of paper found among his things."

"Goes by Jorginsen. Willehelm Jorginsen. Arrived a week ago, as I said. Foreigner. Met with Mr. Dekker, another foreigner. They spoke a few minutes, then Jorginsen asked about a room. Not full up, so I gave him a room across the hall from Dekker."

Hodgins made notes while he listened. "And what did they talk about? Did they know each other?"

"Don't rightly know. Weren't speaking English. German, maybe."

"Dutch, I expect. What else can you tell me? Do you know where either worked?"

Thompson shook his head. "Dekker never spoke of work, but he kept odd hours. He'd leave late in the afternoon and usually came back after dark. Sometimes didn't return until morning. Finally gave him a key. Got fed up being woken to unlock the front door. Been here a month and caused no trouble, so I didn't see the harm."

"Why didn't you just ask him to leave if he couldn't keep proper hours?"

"He always paid on time. More than I can say for some of the others. Like I said, place ain't full. With Willehelm gone, I'll have to find another lodger. Guess I'd best empty his room. Maybe Dekker will want his belongings."

"No, don't touch anything. I'll need to see his room."

The landlord let out a long sigh and headed to the second floor. "This way."

The furnishings were sparse. A small frame bed, a wardrobe with no door, and a washstand with a chipped washbasin, shaving mug and matching brush. The washstand had one crooked door containing under-garments. A travel satchel sat on a two-foot square table, a stark contrast to the rest of the room. The soft leather of the satchel appeared new.

Hodgins opened the bag. "Empty. I'll be taking this with me."

Next, he checked the wardrobe. A white shirt and matching black jacket and trousers hung inside. Nothing else. Hodgins fingered the material. "Expensive. Why would he be staying in a boarding house instead of a hotel? No offence. It looks like he could afford it." He turned to Thompson. "Did you ever hear them speak English?"

"Not really. Only when he inquired about the room. Dekker spoke English to me before Willehelm arrived, but we never sat and chatted. Suppose you want to see Dekker's room, too?"

"Can't search it without cause. It's not against the law to be friends with a murdered man." Hodgins handed him his calling card. "When you see him, ask him to come to Station Four." He smiled. "At a reasonable hour. I'll be taking Jorginsen's things with me."

He packed the few personal items and clothing found in the room into the satchel, then flagged down the first hansom cab he spotted to take him back to the police station.

* * *

When Hodgins arrived, Barnes had already returned and sat waiting, flipping through his notes.

"Sir, I couldn't find any newsagents selling that Brooklyn paper. They all said they didn't know where it could be purchased."

"Don't worry. I didn't expect you'd find one. Can't imagine there's much call for it. Of course, if it was the *New York Daily Times*, everyone would have it and we'd be no further ahead. It's become quite popular."

Barnes glanced at the satchel. "Are you going somewhere?"

"What? Oh. This belongs to the dead man. Willehelm Jorginsen. I tossed in everything I could find in his room. Come with me, and bring a pair of scissors."

Hodgins led Barnes to the interrogation room and sat the case on the table. "We need to carefully check his pockets and all the seams in his other suit. We may just strike gold."

"Maybe diamonds this time." Barnes grinned. "I'll take the jacket."

Hodgins handed it to the constable, and he took the trousers. They worked side-by-side, running their fingers along every seam.

"Looks like the suit he wore held everything." Barnes ran his hand over the lining. "Hold on." Something crinkled. "Hand me the scissors, sir." The constable snipped the hem until he had a big enough space for his hand. He reached in and pulled out another piece of paper. "It's a list of names."

Hodgins took the paper from Barnes. "Some of the names are crossed off. I recognize one of them. A prominent local businessman. Could this be a list of people Jorginsen stole from?"

"Maybe a list of fences for the gems?"

A knock on the door interrupted them. The desk sergeant opened it and stepped in. "Sorry, but you've received a reply from the New York Police." He gave the telegram to the detective and returned to his desk.

CHAPTER SIX

The telegram was brief. Hodgins read it and relayed the contents to Barnes. "A few high-end jewellery stores in New York City were robbed recently. Loose stones taken. Nothing in Brooklyn, though. He's asked me to keep him updated."

Barnes scratched his head. "I'm confused. If the robberies were in New York City, why a Brooklyn newspaper? And this list, it only has individual names, not jewellery stores."

Hodgins considered the information they had. "The newspaper page was found in the alley near the body, not on it. Maybe it's not connected. Wind could have carried it for blocks. Look into the names listed. See if they're local or from New York. I'll look into another Dutchman who's staying at the same boarding house."

The detective headed back downtown to look for his young, reliable informant. It'd been quite some time since he'd seen Backstreet Billy and wasn't sure the lad still ran with the gamblers. He headed for the last location Billy called home. Unfortunately, he found it deserted.

Hodgins tried to get information from the street urchins he'd encountered other times, but many had moved on, and the ones now in the area didn't know Billy. Finally, he found a newspaper hawker who'd worked the corner for a few years and knew both the detective and Billy.

"Afternoon, gov. Newspaper? Latest edition."

Hodgins tossed him a coin and took the paper. "Looking for Billy. He's not at his old spot."

"Nah. Billy's all la-de-dah now. Got hisself a proper room."

"Still working for Stretch? I'd hoped he'd quit by now. Know what boarding house?"

"Ya. Up on Bond Street. Nelson's place. Don't know about Stretch. Heared he moved on."

"I know the place. Glad to hear Stretch has left the city. Thanks Tommy." Hodgins tucked the newspaper under his arm and headed north.

The boarding house sat a few blocks south of Station House Four. A few of the constables boarded there. Hodgins had been to this one before and had always found it clean and well maintained. He smiled as he walked, pleased that young Billy now had a warm, clean place to call home. Much better than the space under a side-entrance porch on a run-down building. Since Billy's employer, Stretch, ran gambling establishments only operating after midnight, there was a good chance Billy would be at home catching up on sleep, unless the paper hawker was correct and Stretch no longer ran gambling houses in the city.

Hodgins stopped in front of the lodgings, taking in the appearance as it'd been a while since he'd visited. The tiny garden in front of the porch bloomed, almost weed-free, and nothing seemed to require repair. He knew the inside was also kept tidy. Nodding his approval of Billy's new home, he walked to the door and knocked.

Only a minute passed before someone clomped down the staircase. Instead of the door opening, the footfalls disappeared towards the back of the house.

He knocked again.

More footfalls. This time, the door opened. A woman in her fifties answered, wearing a cap and apron, suggesting she was the charwoman.

"Good day, Ma'am. Is Mrs. Nelson available?

The woman laughed. "I'm Mrs. Nelson. Just doing a bit of cleaning. Charlady's day off."

"Excuse me for the error. Is Billy in?" For the first time, Hodgins realized he didn't know the lads' family name.

She looked at the badge on his suit jacket. "I've seen you before. He's not in trouble, is he? Such a good boy."

"No, nothing like that. He's an acquaintance. Just checking to see how Billy's getting on."

She cocked her head and gave him the once-over before answering. "He's not home. Got hisself a good job. Come back tonight. Expect you'll find 'im here."

Good. No longer working for Stretch. "Would you be kind enough to tell me where he works?"

"Got a job at the newspaper. Expect he'll be wanting to be called Esquire Miller soon." She let loose a deep belly laugh, showing off her missing bottom tooth.

The detective was taken aback. "The newspaper? You mean *The Globe?*"

"Nah, the other one. Newish.

"The Evening Telegram?" Hodgins knew the paper supported the Conservative party, unlike *The Globe*, owned by George Brown, a supporter of the Liberals.

"Ya, that one. Mind, he sometimes comes in later if he's extra busy."

"Thank you. Tell him Detective Hodgins would like a word, just in case I don't find him. He knows how to reach me."

As he made his way to the newspaper office, Hodgins wondered how Billy managed to land the "good job" and where Stretch went. At least he now knew the lad's full name. William Miller. Hodgins hailed a passing cab to get out of the heat.

The driver pulled the horse to a stop in front of the Melinda Street address eight minutes later. Hodgins went in looking for Billy and spotted someone handing out the mail. He walked over to a lad, likely in his late teens, about the same age as Billy.

"Excuse me. I'm looking for William Miller. Billy. Can you tell me where I could find him?"

"Billy? Sure. Out somewhere. He digs up information for the reporters, so he ain't in the building much."

The detective chuckled. *Exactly what I need him for.* "Is there any way to find out where he might be?"

"Sorry. Everyone keeps their stories close to the vest. Don't want someone else to scoop them."

"Understandable. If you happen to see him, tell him Detective Hodgins is looking for him." With a look of surprise on the young man's face, he waved his hand. "Don't be concerned. Billy's not in trouble. We're friends of sorts. He knows where to find me or to leave a message." Hodgins turned to leave.

"Say, detective. I'm trying to get hired on as a reporter. If I could find a juicy story before anyone else…"

Hodgins studied his face and decided he looked earnest. "Tell you what… I don't know your name."

"Charlie. Charlie Dobbs."

"Tell you what Charlie Dobbs. How about I let you know when we catch the person responsible for murdering the man found by the distillery? Scoop whoever wrote the cover story in Monday's afternoon edition."

Charlie's eyes widened. "Gosh, really?" His shoulders slumped. "Mr. Pirie will probably just hand it over to his best reporter. The one already assigned to it."

"But he'll know you found the information first." Hodgins gave the lad a wink and headed out to find Billy.

Instead of grabbing a hansom back to the police station, he zigzagged his way through the city on foot, inquiring about Billy. Many of the street vendors and hawkers knew the boy, as did some of the children living rough.

When the day began, the detective had a pocket full of coins, a reward for anyone willing to speak with him, as well as those who didn't. He made certain to give them enough to get a good meal. By the time he settled back in his office, his pockets were empty and he'd discovered nothing.

Maybe a nice cup of tea will clear my mind. Hodgins rose and exited his office.

The desk sergeant walked by at the same time. "Oh, yer back. Got a message from that young lad, Billy. Said to meet him at the usual place 'round five."

"Thanks, Cooper." Hodgins checked his pocket watch. "Blimey, it's just gone five. Hope he waits."

Tea forgotten, Hodgins ran out and headed to Mitchell's stable. Instead of hiding in one of the horse stalls like usual, Billy stood in the open, brushing one of the mares.

"Hear yer lookin' fer me." Billy continued brushing.

"Yes. I was pleasantly surprised to learn you aren't running for Stretch any longer. Just wish you could've found something confirming that crooked copper from Station Three was in cahoots before quitting."

"It got too dangerous, and I'd saved a fair bit. Besides, he moved on. Montreal, I think." He glanced at the detective, then back at the horse. "I know you said ya'd help me get a bank account, but my landlady offered. Didn't want ta bother ya."

Hodgins placed a hand on Billy's shoulder. "I'm just glad you're doing well and have a nice place to live."

"Ta. I'm guessing you need my help?"

The detective nodded. "Trying to find out anything about a couple of Dutchmen. They're staying at a boarding house on King Street, a little west of York. Number one fifty-eight. One of them was murdered recently. Clothing had gems hidden in the seams of the first."

Billy nodded. "Know the place. Not as nice as mine. Got a friend with an acquaintance who lives there. Go around sometimes to play poker. I'm gettin' pretty good at it. Last time I was there, I heard some men speaking another language. Could be them. Weren't speaking French. I know that much. Maybe a week ago."

"Sounds like them. Dead man is Jorginsen. Other chap is Hans Dekker. Trying to track him down."

"Ya thinking he kilt 'im?"

Hodgins shrugged. "Maybe, or at least has an idea who did. Someone's definitely going to be looking for the jewels. Don't go spreading that around. Say, now that you're a proper gent, and no longer skulking around, why don't you come and visit us? My wife would like to meet you, and you won't have to worry about word getting back to Stretch you've been seen with a copper."

He looked closely at the ill-fitting jacket Billy wore, and tugged at the lapels. "Maybe she can tailor this a little." Hodgins tore a piece of paper from his notebook and wrote his address. "I'm off Saturday, if you're free. Lunch?"

Billy nodded, grin so big it almost split his face in two.

CHAPTER SEVEN

When Hodgins arrived at the station the next morning, a piece of paper littered his otherwise clean desktop. He picked it up and settled onto his chair to read it. His bottom barely hit the seat before he leapt up and hurried to the sergeant's desk.

"Do you have the report on this?" The detective placed the paper on Cooper's desk.

The sergeant read the note. "I just arrived. Let me check the night log." He opened the logbook and flipped to the last entry. "Here it is. Check Duggan's desk. It was late, so he may not have filed the report."

As Hodgins headed across the room, the front door opened and Barnes came in. A gust of warm summer wind sent a spray of rain behind him.

"Not a fit day for anyone but ducks." Barnes shook out his umbrella and dropped it in the basket kept by the front entrance. "Almost made it here before it started."

"Stand by the potbelly if you can take the heat and try to dry off. Might have to go out again." Hodgins sorted through the piles on Duggan's desk. "How the blazes does that man find anything?"

"Says he has a system, sir." The constable hung his raincoat on a hook, then tried to dry off by the wood stove. "Whew, too hot to wear that coat, but at least my uniform is mostly dry. Whatcha looking for?"

"Someone broke into one of the jewellers on King overnight. Need his notes."

"If it was late, he won't have written a full report. Keeps his book in the top right drawer."

"Got it. Grab a couple of teas and join me in my office." Hodgins flipped to the end of the notes as he walked across the room.

While waiting for Barnes, the detective copied Duggan's scribbles into his own book. When Barnes came in, Hodgins sat rubbing his temples.

"Sir? Is something wrong?" Barnes placed a teacup on the desk and slid it towards the detective.

"Someone broke into the Jewellery Manufacturer at 15 King Street West. Bold bugger. Blew the safe. Duggan was walking down Yonge on his nightly rounds and heard the blast. He spotted a busted window and saw a man in the back office with a satchel, filling it with loose stones. He called out, and the thief closed the satchel and ran out the front door. He wacked Duggan with the satchel, knocking him on his arse. Thief headed down Jorden Street. By the time Duggan got up to chase, the man disappeared."

Barnes perched on the edge of the chair in front of Hodgins' desk. "Is Duggan okay? Did he actually write he landed on his arse?"

"Not in so many words. We can check on him after we go to the jeweller's. Can't help but think it might be connected to the gems sewn in Jorginsen's clothes. No other jewel robberies here, so he must have stolen them before arriving in the city."

Ten minutes later, they exited the station house, each with a black umbrella. As soon as Barnes opened his, a gust of wind turned it inside out. Almost a third of the wooden ribs snapped in half.

Hodgins stood close to the wall, trying to avoid the full force of the storm. "Toss that back inside. It's no good now. I see a hansom coming. I'll flag it down." He took off running as Barnes opened the door and tossed the broken brolly inside.

Despite the brief time outside, both were soaked by the time they settled in the cab. The driver kept the horse moving slowly, as its hooves slipped on the wet cobbles. When they finally arrived and exited at the jeweller's on King Street, the wind blew even stronger, whipping around the buildings. The moment the detective stuck his head out the door, his homburg flew off.

"Dang. That was my best one. Had it nicely broken in. Oh, well." He dashed for the Jewellery Manufacturer's door, Barnes close on his heels. They found the door locked. Hodgins pounded until someone finally answered from inside.

"Go away. We're closed."

"Police. Open up."

"About time." The lock clicked, and the heavy wooden door swung open. The two officers stepped in, dripping water onto the hardwood floor. As the owner shut the door, someone shoved back and entered.

"Bert!" Hodgins recognized one of the hansom drivers.

The cabbie added more rain to the inside of the jeweller's before he managed to close the door. He held out his hand. "Thought you might want this." The detective's homburg hung in Bert's hand, crushed and torn. "Got a mate who's a milliner. Tell 'im I sent ya and you'll get a discount. Got a piece of paper?"

Hodgins handed over his notebook and pencil, taking his hat in exchange. "What are you doing here? Thought you started later in the day." Hodgins put the hat on a nearby table.

"Had a late-night booking. Got paid double to wait. Jest took 'em home now." He handed the notebook and pencil back.

"Don't suppose you were in the area around midnight?"

Bert shook his head, spraying everyone with water. "Sorry. No, my customers were a few blocks away. Snoozed outside under a big maple until they were ready to return. Something happen?"

"My shop's been robbed. At least ten thousand in loose stones taken." The owner's face turned red. He pointed at Hodgins and Barnes. "And these two are just standing there chatting."

"Calm down, sir. One of our constables was here right after it happened." Hodgins flipped his notebook to the pages where he'd copied Duggan's notes. "He saw the man responsible. Got a bit of a description before he was clocked across the head with the thief's satchel. Isn't he the one who contacted you? I don't see your name in the notes."

"Richard Cobb. And no. It was Mr. Morrison from across the road. He was working late, catching up on some special orders, and heard the blast. He spoke to the constable, then came and got me." Cobb calmed a little, lowering his voice. "Now that I think about it, he did have a welt on his temple. Not serious, I hope?"

"Don't believe so. He's our next stop." Hodgins turned to Bert. "Thanks for grabbing my hat. Keep your ears open. Whoever stole them will likely be looking for a buyer."

Bert nodded and left, letting another wet gust swirl inside.

"Have you had a chance to check your inventory? You said ten thousand dollars worth was taken. Do you have a list?" Hodgins looked around the store. "Doesn't appear like any of your displays were ransacked."

"Only the safe." Cobb scratched his balding head. "Strange he busted the front window to get inside. Few doors down's an alley leading to a lane behind these buildings. Could've gone in and out the back without being seen."

"Maybe he doesn't know the area." Barnes' eyebrows shot up. "Sir, could this be connected to—"

The detective held up his hand and shook his head, stopping the constable from blurting anything out, then turned to Cobb. "Another case, but it may be related. I noticed there are a few jewellers within sight of your business. I'll speak with them and advise them to take extra care, just in case. If you'd like, I can have Barnes stay until you get the window replaced, or at least boarded up."

"Appreciate it. The wife's coming to watch the store while I get boards. I came to town with Morrison. Told the missus to follow after feeding our son and leaving him with a neighbour. The constable, Barnes, is it? He can leave when she arrives. Shouldn't be long."

"Sir, if you don't need me to rush anywhere, I don't mind staying to help him board the window."

"That's fine. I'll go chat with the other jewellers, if they're in yet. They should be opening shortly. Suggest they not leave loose stones or expensive jewellery overnight in the shop. I'll collect you when I'm done."

Cobb locked the door as soon as Hodgins left.

***

"I'll stand outside in front of the busted window. People are beginning to stir. Hey!" Barnes hurried to the window. "Off with you." He grabbed the dirty arm of one of the numerous street kids in the city. "Drop it." The lad released the ring and took off as soon as Barnes let go.

Cobb retrieved an empty lock-box from his office and joined Barnes at the broken window. "I'd better pack up the remaining gems and figure out what's missing. Guess I'll have to see about a new safe, too. At least most of my office is intact. One leg of the desk is damaged and a file cabinet got knocked sideways."

Cobb removed everything around the gaping hole, then checked the time. "Hope my wife gets here soon." He unlocked the door so Barnes could go out and stand guard in the rain.

Mrs. Cobb arrived twenty minutes later, bringing a bit of sunshine with her, and handed the reins over to her husband.

She chatted with Barnes for a bit while her husband rode off. "I didn't get all the details when Mr. Robinson came to fetch Richard. Something about an explosion? I was so worried. I do hope no one was hurt."

"Just a broken leg." Barnes grinned at the look on her face. "On a desk. Oh, and a sore head on Constable Duggan. Got knocked down by the thief."

"Gracious! I do hope he's not badly injured." Her eyes widened. She reached for the building as she swayed.

"No ma'am. Sorry. Didn't mean to make light of it. Maybe you should go inside. I'll stay here and guard the store."

A half hour later, Mr. Cobb returned, a load of lumber and nails in the wagon. Together, Barnes and Cobb made a frame to fit the window and nailed boards across it to make a solid wall. They had it almost fastened when Hodgins returned.

Once inside, he surveyed the repair. "That should hold until a replacement glass can be cut." Hodgins spied the constable's helmet and jacket on the end of the counter. "Don't like your uniform any more, Barnes?"

"Sorry, sir. It's just so hot." Barnes wiped the sweat from his brow before reaching for his discarded items. He grinned as he shrugged on the damp jacket. "Just had it cleaned and didn't want to wash it again so soon. Laundry day is not Violet's favourite. I believe we're about finished here."

"Not to worry. Don't blame you for taking it off. Mr. Cobb, when you've completed your inventory, could you drop off a list of stolen items and their value? Station Four on Wilton."

"I should have it shortly. The wife can drop it off on her way home."

CHAPTER EIGHT

Hodgins flagged a passing cabbie to take them to Duggan's home on Church Street to check on him. Once settled, Barnes relayed what Mrs. Cobb had said while they waited for her husband to return with the lumber.

"Based on her husband's mumbling before he took the buggy, she thinks the thief got mostly rubies and sapphires, along with a handful of diamonds. Good thing Duggan was on hand, or the safe would likely be empty. Can't be a coincidence the dead man had a suit full of gemstones and a jewellery store is robbed the next day, can it?"

"Well, it could be, but I doubt it. We need to look into Jorginsen and Dekker. Maybe they have an accomplice here." Hodgins snapped his fingers. "We need a description of Dekker. He may well be the thief."

The hansom stopped, and the driver opened the door. Hodgins paid the fare, then he and Barnes went in to check on Constable Duggan's injuries. Like Barns before his marriage to Violet, Duggan lived with his parents and two siblings. Mrs. Duggan led them to the kitchen.

"Sit and have a cuppa. I won't take no for an answer." Mrs. Duggan placed two cups on the table opposite her son. "Such a brave boy."

Duggan grinned, not at all embarrassed by his mother's fussing. "Ma, I was just doin' my job. The detective needs to speak with me, in private."

Mrs. Duggan mussed his hair. "Such an important job."

"Ma!"

"I'm going. I'm going." She set a plate of fresh biscuits on the table, kissed the top of Duggan's head, then left them alone.

"Gosh. *My* ma thought I had a dangerous job and wished I'd find something else." Barnes took a biscuit and dunked it in his tea.

"She's always fussed over us. Pa's the same. Got over being embarrassed a long time ago. Guess you're here about the robbery?"

"First, how are you?" Hodgins pointed at the bandage wrapped around Duggan's head. It had loosened when his mother mussed his hair. "Expect you'll be off for several days." He sipped the tea and sampled the biscuits while listening to Duggan's reply.

"Nah. It's just a scrape and a bump. Little bruise on my backside, too. As I said, Ma fusses. I'll be back tomorrow."

Hodgins waved a hand. "No, take another day. Already have one injured constable refusing to go home. If you still feel up to it, report Thursday for your normal shift. Now, do you recall anything you didn't put in your notes? Something come to you later?"

Barnes took Duggan's notebook from his pocket and slid it across the table. "We were wondering if the jewel theft might be connected to the murdered man you were called to."

Duggan shrugged. "Couldn't rightly say." He smiled. "Despite the injury, I enjoy the late shift. Streets are nice and quiet, usually. How's a murder connected to a robbery?"

"That's what we're trying to decide. The dead man had jewels on him. A day later, more jewels are stolen. Did the thief say anything to you?" Hodgins turned to Barnes. "How far apart would you say the robbery and murder were?"

"Oh, the theft was clear across town. At least a half hour's walk, if not more. And only a ten-minute walk from the dead man's lodging."

"Well, I do remember one thing." Duggan hesitated. "He mumbled something when he shoved past me, but it was gibberish."

"Gibberish? Could it have been a foreign language?"

Duggan considered it a moment. "Well, at the time, I thought he might have spoken German. Neighbours are German, and I understand a few words, but it didn't really sound right. Is that important?"

"Possibly. The dead man was Dutch. Can you recall what you thought he said?"

"Let me think. Sounded something like old wrapper. Like I said, gibberish."

"Hmm. Barnes, write that down. Maybe Stonehouse will know."

"Old wrapper. Right." The corners of Barnes' mouth turned up. "What's so important about a wrapper?"

"Don't know yet. Anything else before we go?" Hodgins drained his teacup and pushed the chair back, ready to stand.

"No. I'll go over my notes and try to recall. Maybe when my head stops hurting, I can think better."

Mrs. Duggan must have been listening at the door, as she scurried in as soon as she heard the chair scrape across the floor.

"Take care of your lad, Mrs. Duggan. He's a hero." Hodgins turned and winked at the young constable. "Thursday."

CHAPTER NINE

While walking back to the station on Wilton Street, Hodgins and Barnes went over everything they'd learned so far. The constable's stomach growled.

"We'd best stop for a bite to eat before you scare everyone passing by." Hodgins stopped and nudged Barnes. "There's a place near the station. Easier to read our notes sitting." He pointed to the ground as they crossed the road. "Mind the horse droppings."

The detective led Barnes to the Dove Tree Hotel at the corner of Duke and Princess Streets, less than half a dozen blocks south of the station house. Hodgins spotted an empty table by the window. "Over there. Easier to read in the sunlight."

"Sir, I don't believe the Brooklyn paper is important. The telegram from New York said the recent jewel heists were in the city, not Brooklyn. Do we need to follow that up?"

"True, but I don't want to disregard it too soon. The entire paper wasn't in the alley. After lunch, you head to the station. I'll visit the boarding house and have another chat with the landlord. Hopefully, Dekker's finally returned. Maybe someone mailed the newspaper to Jorginsen or Dekker. At the very least, it'd be spotted when cleaning. When you get back, see about having extra patrols along King West, just in case our thief decides to hit the other stores along there. The sergeant can start figuring out which constables to assign, and I'll confirm when I return."

* * *

A young girl, in her early teens, answered the door at the boarding house. "Afternoon, miss. Is Mr. Thompson about?"

"No. Ya just missed 'im. Ya looking fer lodgings? Got a few rooms. Big one just opened up."

He showed his badge. "Need a word about two of his lodgers. Maybe you can help?"

She backed away. "Don't know nuffink. Come in twice a week ta clean." She tried to close the door, but Hodgins put his hand out and gave her his best smile.

"You look about the same age as my daughter, Sara. I hope you can help me with my inquiries. What's your name?"

"Abigail. My friends call me Abby."

"If you'd be more comfortable, we can chat on the porch. Will you help me, Abby?"

She half-hid behind the door. "Ya really got a daughter?"

He nodded. "Yes. Three actually. Have a set of twin girls. They're only three."

49

Abby gave him a good look over, then eased out from behind the door, leaving it open. She stepped out. "Don't know what I kin help with."

Hodgins leaned against the post at the top of the steps. "Newspapers. Do you recall ever seeing a newspaper from Brooklyn, New York? Maybe Mr. Jorginsen or Mr. Dekker had one?"

Her eyes widened. "Paper all the way from New York?"

"Yes, all the way from New York. Did you ever see one in the trash, or maybe in their rooms while cleaning?"

She shook her head.

"Did you see a letter with funny writing on it? Probably Dutch."

Again, she shook her head.

"No newspapers or letters, eh? That's all I wanted to know. Thank you, Abby. You've been a great help." He tipped his homburg and left the shade of the porch. *Blasted heat.*

By the time the detective arrived back at the police station, his shirt clung to his body. By comparison, the inside of Station House Four felt cool. He stopped to speak with the sergeant, wiping his brow with his handkerchief. "Did Henry tell you I'd like the jewellers on King checked frequently at night?"

Sergeant Cooper held up a piece of paper. "All done. Instructions for the evening shift, if the inspector approves. Do you think the thief would be brazen enough to try again?"

"Possibly. A lot of stupid thieves in the city. He was dim enough to blow the safe and think no one would hear. Maybe have the extra patrols for a week. Might be enough to scare him off. With luck, we'll have caught him by then." Hodgins continued to his office, struggling out of his damp suit jacket along the way.

Before he could sit, Barnes came in. "Any luck at the boarding house?"

"Afraid not. There's a cleaning girl there today. Said she never saw any Brooklyn papers while doing her chores. As you said, may not be relevant."

"What's next, sir?"

"We know the man found outside Gooderham's was Jorginsen, a Dutchman. Both he and fellow Dutchman Dekker, lodged at 158 King Street West. According to Duggan's comment, the thief at the jewellery store may have spoken Dutch. I'll go to the morgue to see Stonehouse before heading home. Want to see if 'old wrapper' sounds similar to any word he remembers."

"Funny sounding language, that Dutch."

Hodgins chuckled. "Imagine they think the same about English."

"Say, could they have come into the city from Holland Landing? Sounds like a perfect location."

"Yes, it does. However, it wasn't named after the country. It was named after Samuel Holland, a surveyor. But he was Dutch, so it may be a good place to ask around. Could be some immigrants went there based on the name. All the leads thus far have resulted in nothing, so it wouldn't hurt to make the trip. Better than sitting around on my arse all day. I'll catch the train first thing tomorrow."

CHAPTER TEN

After consulting the Northern Rail schedule, Hodgins was pleased to discover the train didn't depart quite as early as expected. When he woke the next morning, his wife, Cordelia, already had breakfast started.

"Nothing like a full belly to get a man going for the day." He kissed her cheek. "What have you planned for the girls?"

"Sara's going swimming with her friend Lucy. The Mortons have been invited to spend the day at the Howard's and have invited Sara to join them. They have a lovely pond. I believe they call it Grenadier Pond. Amelia is bringing the twin's brother over to play with them while Sara is away."

Hodgins poured two cups of tea, placing one on the counter beside Delia. "I'm glad the twins are getting along with their little brother. Few more years and I suppose we'll all have to sit to discuss how to tell them they're siblings and why they don't live together."

"Years away yet. I just hope by then most folk around here will have forgotten their natural parents were thieves and murderers. Now, sit and eat, or you'll miss your train. Will you be back late?"

The detective took a second plate and set it by the one his wife had placed on the kitchen table. "You've made enough for two. Take advantage while the house is quiet. And no, I doubt I'll be late. I intend to catch the 12:58 train back and should be at the station house before four. If anything holds me up, I'll send a telegram to let you know." He patted the chair seat. "Now sit."

* * *

Hodgins arrived at Union Station with enough time to purchase the early edition of *The Globe* and his train ticket before the incoming train whistle blew. He became engrossed in the article about the murder in Ireland of seventeen-year-old Mary McShane and almost missed the train.

The ride up took over two hours. His long legs cramped, despite several attempts to stroll the length of the train car. The few people around him had no interest in chatting, so he re-read the newspaper, focusing on the Police Court column, then stared out the window.

When the train finally pulled into the station, the detective took a long walk to work the kinks out of his legs. The roar of rushing water drew his interest. Hoping for a lovely river view, and possibly a cooler temperature, he walked over to Chapman Street, heading west towards the rumble. The unmistakable stench of a tannery assaulted him as he crossed a bridge. Covering his nose, he turned up Queen Street to get away from the smell.

The area appeared to be mostly farms, with only a few stores. He found the post office and figured they would know, or at least be somewhat familiar with, the residents.

"Despite the name, the town doesn't have a large Dutch population. 'Fraid you've made the trip for nothing."

Hodgins nodded. "I expected as much, but had to check. And I don't agree the trip to be a waste. It's nice to get out of the city from time to time. As long as I'm here, do the names Jorginsen and Dekker sound familiar?"

"No. We have a family named Vanderplaats just outside town. Good-sized farm, too. You looking for friends of yours?"

Hodgins hesitated, trying to decide what to say. He settled on the truth and introduced himself. "Unfortunately, Mr. Jorginsen has met with foul play. Wondered if maybe he had family around. He lodged at the same place as Dekker, who we can't locate. If you hear anyone mention either name, please have word sent. The stationmaster can relay the message. We'll pay any cost at my end."

With little else to do, the detective found the local store and purchased two dolls for the twins, a little summer hat for Sara, and white dress-gloves for Cordelia. The merchant suggested the Central Hotel, where Hodgins could get an early lunch before heading back to the train.

* * *

When the detective returned to Station House Four, no one had any new information about the murderer or jewel thief. Hodgins dropped his purchases on his desk, then went over to chat with Barnes.

"Henry, we must be missing something. We've had one jewellery store robbed and a man with gems sewn into his clothing murdered. They must be connected. And what about Dekker? It's no coincidence two Dutchmen lived in the same building and didn't know each other previously. Question is, did Dekker introduce Jorginsen to the landlord because he knew him, or simply because he spoke Dutch? Oh, and I spoke to Stonehouse about 'old wrapper'. He spelled it out for me after he finished laughing." Hodgins flipped through his notebook. "Here. *Oelewapper.* Loosely translates to nincompoop, simpleton, clumsy. You get the idea."

Barnes grinned. "Best not let Duggan hear that."

"Doubt he'd be bothered. Seems to have a good sense of humour." Hodgins checked his pocket watch. "Still a few hours left on your shift. Since you've shown what an artist you are, head to the boarding house and get a description of Dekker and make a drawing. I'll try to determine our next course of action. Just wish I had more to go on."

CHAPTER ELEVEN

Hodgins arrived at the station earlier than usual the next morning. Despite the sun barely cresting the horizon, the August temperatures rose higher than normal, with the added bonus of stifling humidity. By the time he reached his office, his sweat-soaked shirt clung to his body again. He'd removed his jacket a few blocks from the station, and fanned his face with his homburg. It hadn't helped.

As he entered his office, he spotted a single sheet of paper sitting dead centre on his desk. Instead of hanging the jacket on the hook beside the door, he flung it towards the empty guest chair and reached for the paper.

"Nicely done, Henry." He examined the detailed drawing, trying to recall if he'd seen the man before. Hodgins rounded his desk and sat, leaning back until the chair groaned.

"So, that's what you look like, Mr. Dekker. Don't suppose you care to tell me what you're doing in my city?"

"You asking me, sir?"

Hodgins looked up. One of the new constables stood at his doorway.

"No." He turned the paper to show the drawing. "Just talking to my friend here." Hodgins chuckled at the lad's puzzled look. "Don't worry. You'll get used to me and my habits if you stick around long enough. You coming in or heading home?"

"In. I have an interest in photography and wanted to check out what we have." The young constable shuffled his feet. "Is that all right? Am I in trouble?"

"Not at all. Always glad to have more than one person with a special skill. Chat with Barnes or Riddell when you have time. You know where the equipment is?"

The constable nodded.

"Good. Mind the chemicals."

"Yes, sir. Thank you."

Hodgins went back to the sketch as the new recruit hurried away. "So, Mr. Dekker, how'd you like to have your picture in the newspaper? I wonder…"

He headed to the back, drawing in hand. The door to the former storage room turned photography room stood open. Hodgins knocked to get the lad's attention.

"Sorry, Constable, but I don't know your name."

"Jones, sir. My friends call me Jonesy."

"You said you have an interest in photography. Do you know how to work a camera?"

"Oh, yes. I'm friends with J.W. Fenner. He's a photographer on Yonge Street. Been giving me tips and letting me use one of his cameras. Haven't done any developing yet, though."

"Oh, that's too bad, but you can at least start until Barnes arrives." He handed Jonesy the sketch. "Can you take a picture of this? I want to get it in the next edition of *The Globe*. You can watch while Henry develops it."

Jonesy puffed out his chest. "Yes, sir. Thank you. I'll be glad to help." He looked around. "I see the camera, but not the tripod."

"Riddell's mother made a carrying bag for it. Look around. Shouldn't be difficult to find. I'll send Barnes back when I see him. Expect he'll arrive shortly."

Hodgins headed to his office as the front door opened. "Barnes, got a new assignment for you. Do you know the new lad? Jones?"

"In passing. You aren't going to have me train him, are you?" The smile he came in with quickly vanished.

"Yes, but not in the way you're thinking. He's interested in photography. Got him taking a photo of your drawing. Good job, by the way. Very detailed. I'd like to get it in *The Globe*. Seems Jones is experienced taking pictures, but hasn't learned how to develop them. Go back and show him how it's done, then he can run it to the paper. I'll write up something while you're getting it ready."

"Gladly. Always happy to keep my hands in it, so to speak. Don't get as many opportunities now that Tom knows what he's doing."

Twenty minutes later, Barnes and Jones stepped into the detective's office with not one, but two copies of the sketch. "Don't tell Tom, but Jonesy caught on faster. There's going to be competition between them."

Jonesy stammered. "I, um, well…

"Don't fret, Jones. Riddell will enjoy having a competitor other than Barnes. And you had a head start. Riddell got thrown into it. Now, do you know where *The Globe* office is?"

"Sure. At King and Jordan."

"Right. Take one of those copies and this." Hodgins handed him a sheet from his pad of foolscap. "Ask them to run this for a couple of days. All editions. Hopefully, someone recognizes him and contacts us."

"Right away." Jonesy took off running.

"Eager lad." Barnes lifted Hodgins' damp jacket off the chair and hung it up before sitting. "What's next?"

"Not certain. We usually have several people to interview and one or two leads to follow. The connection to New York hasn't panned out. We don't have a description of the man who robbed the jeweller, except that he's likely Dutch The only other Dutchman we know about is missing. I'm certain he must be connected to the dead man. I don't recall how long the char girl said they've been at the boarding house. Dekker's been there longer, though. Jorginsen's room looked like he'd settled in. I think the landlord said about a week."

"Don't know about him, but Dekker's been there over a month. Found that out when making the sketch. Both the landlord and maid mentioned they'd seen him enough over the past few weeks to give me a good description." Barnes pointed at the drawing. "Even noticed the cut on his ear. Said it was fresh when he first came in. Sounds like it was bad enough to leave a scar. That's why I included it."

"Why don't you make a dozen more copies of this and Riddell's photo of the dead man? I'll take one of each to the docks and ask around. You head to Union Station and see if anyone remembers a Dutchman arriving a few weeks ago. Distribute the rest and have the men ask around while on the beat. Oh, and take a photo of the sketch you made at Gooderham's. Do that first. I'd like to take it with me. Have another look around while I'm down there."

By half-past nine, Hodgins snooped around the alley where Jorginsen's body was discovered. Not much had changed since Monday, just different litter, and the crates and barrels rearranged. Since there'd been no word from the distillery, he made his way to the office. A middle-aged man sat at a desk outside the main offices. The open doors let Hodgins know neither Gooderham nor Worts was in.

"Can I help you?" The man rose from his chair and approached the detective.

"You must be his clerk." Hodgins nodded towards Gooderham's office, trying to hide his surprise at the man's height. He towered over Hodgins, who always had to look down at people.

"David Bowdre. I assist both Gooderham and Worts. Are you here to place an order?"

"No." Hodgins extended his hand and introduced himself.

"Ah. You're here about the dead man. I put up a notice in each building, but all of our employees are accounted for."

"I see. I don't suppose you have any Dutchmen here? I have a likeness." He showed the clerk the photograph of both the dead man and Barnes' sketch of Dekker.

"Sorry, but I'm not familiar with many of the workers." He glanced at the photographs. "No, I don't believe I've seen either before."

"Thank you for your time. I need these copies, but I'll have a constable bring down more and go through your buildings to show them." As Hodgins turned to leave, he noticed a newspaper on a small table near the door. He picked it up and turned back. "Someone here reads *The Brooklyn Daily Eagle?*"

"Yes, that's mine. I used to live there and like to keep current. I've been saving so I can return. My parents are still there and aging."

"Family obligations. I understand. Good day, sir." He put the newspaper back and headed to the docks.

CHAPTER TWELVE

Several ships were docked, but one ship had gotten an early start on its journey. By the time Hodgins reached the pier, it had sailed almost a mile out. Fortunately, the adjacent piers still had merchant vessels moored. Several longshoremen carried steamer trunks up the gangplank, avoiding collisions with the others using small carts. Yelling farther down the shore caught Hodgins' attention. A cargo net dangled from three corners. The fourth had given way, the contents spilling onto the pier.

Figuring the man yelling must be in charge, the detective strolled over, avoiding the damaged contents and broken crates.

"I see it's a bad time, but I only need a moment." He showed his badge. "Just need you to look at these photographs. Have you seen either man?" Hodgins held out the photos.

"Ain't seen 'im. Baxter, get this mess cleaned up or I'll keelhaul ya."

"Sir, if you'd just take a moment to look." Hodgins practically shoved the print in the man's face. "They're Dutch."

"If it'll git rid of ya. Dutch, eh? Ain't seen 'im. Try down there. Two ships over. Have a lot of foreigners." The longshoreman stomped away before Hodgins could respond.

A large schooner rocked on the low waves, and few sailors milled around. *Sails are still down. Not ready to pull anchor yet.* As Hodgins made his way over, he showed the photograph to everyone who would stop. Shrugs and shaken heads, accompanied by the occasional foreign word, were most of the replies. The answers he received in English were words he wouldn't even repeat to his closest friends.

Not one person would admit to seeing Dekker or Jorgenson. He noted expressions as each person saw the photos. Not a glimmer of recognition. *I hope Barnes has better luck at the train station.*

Hodgins made it to the Sherbourne Street docks before turning up Sherbourne, heading north until he spotted a hansom to take him to the police station. When he arrived, Barnes hadn't returned yet.

"Detective, there you are." The desk sergeant exited from the back. "About a half hour ago, we got a report of another robbery." Sergeant Cooper returned to his desk and checked the logbook. "Mr. Morrison, 14 King Street West. Another jeweller. Came in to open up and found the back door busted open. Details are on your desk. Thought it might be connected to the other."

"Blast! Across the street from the first and only two days later. Brazen chap, if it's the same person. What happened to the extra patrols?"

"Couldn't change the schedule that fast. And when I say details, well, bit of an exaggeration." Cooper shrugged. "Morrison's expecting a visit from someone other than a constable."

Hodgins grumbled a thanks and went to his office. One sheet of paper lay on his desk. Only three lines were written on it. Morrison's name, store address, and the words *jewel theft*.

"Details indeed." He folded the paper and stuck it between the pages of his notebook, then headed down to King Street.

* * *

"Took your bloody time!" Morrison barely glanced at Hodgins' badge. "First Cobb, now me. Who's next? What are you going to do? We need protection."

"I've arranged for dedicated nightly patrols, but they won't start until tonight. I'll need a list of what was taken. Was anyone here when it happened?"

"No. I've already spoken to the other jewellers on the street. We're hiring someone to keep an eye on the block. Maybe two if we can afford it. Cheaper than losing our stock. They'll be armed. God help anyone trying it again."

"Mr. Morrison, please leave this to the police. By all means, hire night guards, but no weapons. I don't believe the thief is dangerous. He had the opportunity to attack one of my constables and only pushed past him. If someone is shot, you'll be held accountable."

"We got a right to protect our property. Do something, or we will."

Hodgins took a deep breath to calm his rising temper. "Mr. Morrison, if you'll just give me the information I need, we'll track down the person responsible. Where did he gain entry? Back door, I believe? Show me."

"Through here." Morrison led the detective into an office. The back door stood wide open, hanging by the top hinge.

"Someone must have heard when the door broke. Had to have taken considerable force to bust it like that." Hodgins stepped outside and looked around. A light shone through an upstairs window next door.

Morrison followed his gaze. "Arthur must be up. Lives above his shop."

"Maybe he heard or saw something. I'll have a word with him when I finish here."

"You'll have to wait until he opens. Won't unlock the door so much as a minute early." Morrison checked the time. "Ten minutes, not a second earlier."

Hodgins sighed. "I can wait. Does your store have an upstairs flat, too? May I see it?"

"Using it for storage."

Hodgins said nothing, staring at Morrison, waiting for permission to go into the loft.

"Suit yurself." He stepped back inside and opened a door off to the right, revealing a stairwell.

Hodgins started up. "Do you keep the office and back doors locked during the day?"

"Back door's locked. I go in and out of my office all day. Can't be doing with locking and unlocking. Does it matter?"

Hodgins stood at the top of the stairs. The area was large enough for a single person to be quite comfortable. A bedframe leaned against the far wall, waiting to be reassembled. Several large items lay hidden under white sheets. *Furnishings?* Everything was covered with a thick layer of dust.

"Mr. Morrison, is it possible someone snuck into your office and hid up here?"

Morrison climbed halfway up. "Find something?"

"Footprints. Surprised you didn't hear him sneeze, what with all this dust." Hodgins started down, waving at Morrison to do the same.

"But the door? Someone broke in."

"No. I think it likely he broke out. If you won't lock the office door, I suggest you install a strong lock on the loft door." Hodgins checked his pocket watch. "Ten minutes is almost up. If you wouldn't mind listing everything that was stolen, I'll go next door and wait for Arthur to open. Oh, if you can recall the customers in the shop, I'll need that list, too. Drop it off at Station Four, Wilton Avenue."

Hodgins stood outside the barbershop next door, pocket watch in hand. Arthur unlocked the door just as the hands reached 10:00 a.m.

"Come in, young man. First customer of the day."

Arthur sported a full, bushy beard, an odd contrast to his shiny, bald head. Hodgins pointed to Arthur's moustache, then his own. Both sported handlebar mustaches, waxed into a tight curl. Arthur won for size as his was at least an inch longer at the tips.

"Afraid I'm not a cust—"

"Sit. Any chair you'd like." Arthur removed Hodgins' homburg and directed him to the closest chair. "I see you've decided to go against most men and not grow a beard. Very nice 'tache you've got, even if it's not as grand as mine. Just the right amount of curl on the tips."

Hodgins laughed, but sat as directed. "I'm not here for a haircut." He introduced himself as he looked in the mirror. "Guess I could use a trim. Can you talk and cut at the same time?"

"That's my specialty. What would you like to talk about?" Arthur draped a cloth around the detective, then picked up a pair of hand-forged scissors.

"Theft next door last night. Don't suppose you heard or saw anyone? Just tidy up the ends " Hodgins watched as Arthur skillfully worked the scissors, stopping regularly to sharpen them on a leather strap.

"Next door? West side's a vacant lot, so you must mean Charlie. Didn't hear a thing. Wear earplugs at night. Saloon down the way gets awful noisy. Charlie's not hurt, is he?"

Arthur stopped cutting and brushed all around Hodgins' neck, removing the fragments of hair.

"No, he's fine. Just lost merchandise and will have to replace his back door."

Arthur held a mirror so Hodgins could see the back. "That do ya?"

"Yes. My wife will appreciate it. Thank you." The detective took a handful of coins from his pocket and dropped several on the small shelf in front of the wall mirror, and started for the door.

"Hold on. That's more than double the cost." Arthur picked up some of the coins and held them out.

"Worth every penny. Good day." Hodgins put his homburg back on and headed out.

As he walked past Morrison's, the jeweller waved him in. "Here's the list you wanted. I remembered something as I made it out. One customer in particular. Not a regular. Didn't say much, just looked at everything. Had some sort of accent. Broken English. Strange thing is, I don't recall him leaving. Course, he coulda left when I was busy with Mrs. Anderson. Difficult woman to please, but she spends plenty in the end."

"Blast! Must have left the photographs in the hansom cab." He snapped his fingers. "*The Globe* should be running a copy of the sketch in the next few editions. Take a look and let me know if that's the man you saw. Better yet, I'll find a hawker or newsstand and purchase a copy." Hodgins hurried out, expecting to find a newsboy at or near the corner.

Less than five minutes later, he returned, interrupting an exchange with a customer. "Excuse me. Is this the man?" Hodgins held up the newspaper with the photograph of Dekker.

"Yes, that's him."

Hodgins left the paper on a display case on the way out and grabbed the northbound trolley just as it approached King. When he exited near the station, he ran the dozen blocks to Station House Four, sweat stinging his eyes.

CHAPTER THIRTEEN

The rest of the day progressed painfully slow. They still had no idea where Dekker was, and he hadn't returned to the boarding house. Everything pointed to him being the thief, but so far, Hodgins had no concrete evidence to prove it. *Could he have killed his friend, too?* Hodgins read and re-read the notes, but nothing jumped out.

Discouraged, the detective shoved his notebook into his jacket pocket and headed out, stopping at Cooper's desk. "Gotta clear my head. I'll be at the Horticultural Gardens on Gerrard for a bit, then home, if anything comes up."

Walking slower than usual, it took almost twenty minutes to cover the short distance. He rambled the grounds, finally entering the three-story pavilion. With the building designed to keep the plants warm during the winter, the temperature became unbearable.

Hodgins removed his jacket and headed to the exit. He found an empty bench under the shade of a large maple and sat to gather his thoughts.

By the time Hodgins left, he felt relaxed, even though he'd made no new revelations about the case. During his brief time under the tree, dark clouds had covered the sky, blocking some of the sun and heat. Enjoying his stroll, he continued home, arriving just as his eldest daughter, Sara, set the table for their evening meal.

"Good evening, Papa. You look tired. Were you chasing that jewel thief? Did you really see all those pretty stones? Tell me all about it." She took her father's hand and led him to the sitting room. "Oh, I'd love to have all that sparkly jewellery."

"Slow down, Sara. Yes, I am tired, but unfortunately, it's not from chasing a thief. Chasing my tail, more like. Let me sit a spell. You go help your mother with supper.

"No need to help me." Cordelia stood in the doorway. "Everything's ready. Do you think you can manage to walk to the kitchen?"

He stood. "For your cooking, I'd drag myself clear across the city."

Looking around, he noticed the absence of the twins, making their meal unusually quiet. "What have you done with Holly and Ivy? And where's Scraps?"

"They fussed all day because of the heat. Finally managed to get them sleeping. Scraps is upstairs guarding them. He doesn't like the heat either. I'll see if they'll eat when they wake. I have a treat for dessert. Actually, it's Sara's treat." Cordelia nodded at their daughter, who immediately ran to the icebox.

Sara reached in and removed one of her mother's mixing bowls. "Look, Papa. Ice cream. Took forever to make enough. It's lemon-orange, with a few crushed walnuts to sprinkle on top."

"My, you've been busy. Your arm must be sore from all that cranking." Hodgins took a spoonful. "Delicious."

"Mama had to crack the walnuts. Do you really like it?"

"Yes. Just what I needed. It's going to be hard to leave some for the twins." She placed it back in the ice box and sat at the table for dinner.

While they enjoyed their after-dinner treat, Hodgins went over what he'd seen at the jewellery store to a wide-eyed Sara.

"What about the man who died in the whisky?"

"Sara!" Cordelia seemed shocked her daughter knew about that.

"What's wrong, Mama? Papa always talks about his murders."

Hodgins stifled a laugh. "They're not my murders, dear. You make me sound like a killer. And he didn't die in the whisky." He explained as best he could. Nothing seemed to faze Cordelia, and apparently their daughter took after her mother.

Upstairs, one of the twins called out, waking the other. Scraps joined in.

"Sara, please help them down while I prepare a plate for them."

"Yes, Mama." She slipped off the chair and headed upstairs.

"Gracious. The things that girl says. Don't know where she gets it from." Cordelia cleared the table and set two places for the twins.

"Look in the mirror, Delia." Hodgins put the remainder of the ice cream back in the icebox, ducking a swat from his wife.

"So, you've no idea who killed him and stuffed him in the barrel? How sad."

"Nothing confirmed, but I believe his murder is somehow connected to the thefts. Either robbed some store out of town, or it hasn't been reported. Still haven't found the other Dutchman from the boarding house. Makes me wonder if he's responsible."

Cordelia dished out a small amount of cold ham and carrots. "Maybe he's hiding from whoever killed his friend. Now hush. The wee ones are here."

After the twins were fed and the dog given the empty ice cream bowl to lick, Hodgins took the shaggy mongrel for a walk. "So, Scraps. Do you think Dekker murdered Jorginsen?"

"Woof."

"I agree. Murdered his friend, didn't know about the hidden gems, robbed two jewellery stores, and made off. Just wish I knew where he went."

Halfway around the block, shoe leather smacked the ground behind him. Hodgins turned. A constable ran towards him, calling his name.

"Detective Hodgins, finally. There's been another murder." The constable took several deep breaths. "Constable Barnes is on his way to the coroner's."

CHAPTER FOURTEEN

After Hodgins raced home with the dog, he made his way to the morgue. Barnes stood outside, waiting.

"Henry, why were we summoned? Couldn't someone else have dealt with it? You'd think we were the only policemen in the city."

"Doctor Stonehouse wanted to wait for you. Let's get this over with so I can go back home."

Hodgins clapped Barnes on the shoulder. "I'm with you. Come on."

"Gentlemen, sorry to disturb your evening, but I thought you'd want to know about this." Stonehouse held a newspaper in one hand, uncovering the corpse with the other. He held the paper beside the man's face. "Look familiar?"

At the same time, Hodgins and Barnes exclaimed, "Dekker!" Like Jorginsen, Dekker had multiple stab wounds on his neck.

"Please don't tell me he was found in a whisky barrel, too?" Hodgins looked from the newspaper to the dead man. "Strong resemblance."

"Body was found behind the United Empire Club."

"On King Street?" Hodgins turned to the constable. "Not far from the boarding house where the Dutchmen resided. You did an excellent job with your sketch."

"Thank you. And the club isn't far from the jewellery store robberies. I suppose this means Dekker didn't kill his friend?"

"I don't suppose he did, seeing as they appear to have been killed in the same manner. Nothing we can do tonight. First thing tomorrow, we'll need a photograph to take to the boarding house to confirm he's Dekker. Will the body be ready, Doctor?"

"I'll clean him up before I leave, so he'll be presentable."

"Thank you. Come on, Henry. We can share a hansom, if we can find one.

* * *

Riddell came in the next morning while Hodgins updated his notes. "Don't get comfortable, Tom. I need you to go to the morgue with the camera. Stonehouse is expecting you."

By the time Riddell returned and developed the plate, over an hour had passed. The detective took the print and headed to the boarding house.

Abby swept the porch as he approached.

"Good morning, Abby. Remember me?"

"Yeah. Yer the detective with the twins. Mr. Dekker still hasn't returned. Imagine, paying a month in advance and not showing up for his meal and bed."

Hodgins smiled. "Yes, imagine that. Waste of good money. If I showed you a photograph, could you tell me if you recognize the man?"

"Course I can. I got a good memory."

The detective showed the young char girl the photo Riddell had developed.

"That's Mr. Dekker." She examined the print closely before handing it back. "He's not sleeping, is he?"

"No, Abby. Not sleeping."

"Gosh. Mr. Thompson ain't gonna be happy. Two lodgers murdered. He was killed, weren't he?"

Hodgins held back a laugh as he recalled Sara's response at dinner the previous evening. "You are so much like my eldest, Sara. Very inquisitive and straight to the point. Yes, he was murdered, too. Is Mr. Thompson in?"

"Having breakfast. I'll fetch 'im." She grinned. "*You* can tell him he's lost another lodger."

He followed Abby inside and waited while she went to find her employer. Hodgins raised an eyebrow at the bits of conversation filtering down the hall.

"Tell him he can bloody well wait until I've finished my meal. Barely gone nine. Who calls this early? Out with you."

Abby hurried down the hall, a little flustered.

"I heard. It's a nice morning. I'll sit in that lovely wicker rocker on the porch. Don't have many opportunities to do that."

"How about a cuppa and a slice of bread? Fresh baked."

"Don't mind if I do."

Abby returned a few minutes later with a tray, setting it on the small table by the rocker.

"Brought milk and sugar, if'n ya want it, and strawberry jam. One of the ladies down the street makes it. Real good. Not too sweet."

"Thank you. I feel like I'm on holiday. Is Mr. Thompson as upset as he sounded?"

"Nah. Once his belly's full, he'll be in a good mood. At least until he finds out why yer here." Abby gave a small curtsy and went back to her chores.

Hodgins was on his second cuppa when Mr. Thompson came out, wearing another ill-fitting suit, this time in blue.

"I see that girl's been generous with my food."

"Always a good idea to keep the local constabulary happy." The detective pulled the photograph from his jacket pocket. "Abby said she recognized this man as Mr. Dekker. Can you confirm?"

"Damnation! Another one? Yes, that's Dekker. That's it. No more foreigners. Can't understand a damn thing they're saying. Load of crooks."

"We don't know they're crooks, Mr. Thompson. And weren't your parents or grandparents foreigners when they arrived, as were mine? Could be perfectly legitimate businessmen. We're still trying to find out more about them. I'll need to see his room."

Thompson huffed, then mumbled as he led Hodgins back inside. "At least he paid in advance."

The landlord let Hodgins into Dekker's room. It was just as sparse as Jorginsen's.

"Take what ya want. I got no use for anything."

"I'll have a look around, then send one of my constables back for his possessions."

When Thompson left, Hodgins began his search. The wardrobe contained two suits, three white shirts, and a small suitcase. He ran his hands over the clothing, feeling for lumps. Nothing.

He then moved to the desk. The top was clear, but Hodgins found several letters in the drawer. He took those, hoping to find someone who could translate. A shelf above the washstand held a hairbrush, shaving razor with brush, and a small glass with a toothbrush inside.

The letters seemed to be the only items of interest. Hodgins tucked them in his suit jacket pocket with the photograph, and strolled to the station, using the time to mull over the two deceased Dutchmen.

Hodgins walked along Alice Street, eventually making his way to Trinity Church. He sat on the church steps and pulled out his notebook to list his questions.

- Why were jewels sewn into Jorginsen's suit and where did they come from?
- Is it a coincidence Dekker and Jorginsen boarded at the same place?
- Are the recent jewellery store robberies connected?
- Is there significance to the method of death?
- Is there a reason Dekker's body was left at the United Loyalist Club?
- One killer with two knives, or two killers?

"Can I help you?"

Someone behind him spoke, startling him. "Not unless you speak Dutch." Hodgins turned, standing quickly. "Father! Sorry. Just needed a place to collect my thoughts."

"You chose a good location. I'm the rector here. William Darling." He extended his hand. "If you're troubled, come inside."

Hodgins laughed. "I'm with the Toronto Constabulary. Just trying to make sense of some things."

"I see. You're welcome to stop by anytime. Sorry, I don't speak Dutch." The rector smiled and went back in.

Feeling more frustrated than before, the detective snapped his notebook closed and rammed it into his pocket with enough force to tear the seams. "Blast. Delia will have my hide."

He mumbled as he made his way to the police station. "Another dead man. No idea who they are, except for their names, hidden gems, and jewellery robberies. How are they connected? Are they connected?" Hodgins stopped short when he heard his name.

"Detective Hodgins? Did you confirm the dead man is Dekker?" Barnes stood on the step in front of the station.

"What? Yes, it's Dekker." Hodgins looked around. "Guess I'm a little distracted. Walked right past the station. Come into my office and go over everything with me."

Barnes held the door and followed the detective to his office. Once settled, they reviewed everything they'd found, which wasn't much.

"There has to be a connection." Barnes leaned back in the chair.

"I agree, but what is it? We've no proof, and no one to arrest." Hodgins reached into his jacket pocket. "Found a couple of letters in Dekker's room. Unfortunately, they're in Dutch. Not many Dutchmen have immigrated here. Where will I find someone to translate?"

Barnes snapped his fingers. "There's something in yesterday's paper about a visitor from Amsterdam." Henry hurried to his desk and scanned the news as he made his way back to the detective's office.

"Here it is. A visiting professor from the University of Amsterdam is lecturing at the University of Toronto on Dutch painters." He placed the newspaper on Hodgins' desk. "Says it's part of a summer program on art history. Next month, someone's speaking about Italian artists."

Hodgins read the article. "Interesting. He's lecturing tomorrow afternoon, and again Sunday. Only fifty cents per ticket. I'll go to the university today and see if I can speak with him. You grab Harrington and gather up all of Dekker's belongings. Examine them thoroughly."

CHAPTER FIFTEEN

Hodgins made his way to the administration building at the university. The woman behind the desk recognized him at once.

"Detective? Please don't tell me another student has been murdered."

"No. Nothing like that. I'm actually here about the visiting professor. Could you tell me where I might find him? I'd like his help with something."

"The dean is showing him around the grounds. You're welcome to wait."

Hodgins took a flyer from her desk, outlining the planned lectures for the summer, then sat on one of the hard, wooden chairs lined up against the wall.

"Are you interested in art, detective?"

"Only in passing. My daughter enjoys painting. Do you think the lecture would be too advanced for an eleven-year-old?"

She smiled. "I'm guessing she's advanced for her age?"

"Well, sometimes. I've been told she has talent." Hodgins shrugged. "I've not got the education to say."

The door opened, cutting the conversation short. Dean Wilson entered with another gentleman. The secretary nodded in Hodgins' direction.

Hodgins stood. "Detective Hodgins. Could I have a word with your guest? It's rather important."

"Mr. DeWijs is very busy. Can it wait? We were about to attend a luncheon, then he needs to prepare for tomorrow's lecture."

"I understand, but it's police business. I need some letters translated."

Mr. DeWijs spoke up. "As Dean Wilson said, I am very busy, but if important, leave letters and I'll look at them tonight. Would that be *aangenaam*? Agreeable?"

Hodgins hesitated, assessing the foreign visitor. *Nothing suspicious about his mannerisms. Seems pleasant. My gut says he's trustworthy.* "Well, these is our only copies, but yes. I can leave them with you. I plan on attending tomorrow's lecture. Could we speak after?"

"*Ja*. After lecture."

Hodgins shook hands with both men, handed the envelopes to DeWijs, tipped his homburg at the administrative secretary, and made his way back to the station. Remembering his invitation to young Billy, he cursed himself. *Have to make his visit short, unfortunately.*

* * *

When Hodgins arrived, Cooper informed him Barnes and Harrington were in the interrogation room with Dekker's belongings. When he entered, the constables sifted over the clothing.

"Find anything?"

Harrington picked up a small piece of paper from the table. "Part of a note. It's been torn, and we haven't found the rest."

Hodgins took the scrap and read the partial words. "King Stre—. An address for one of the jewellers that was robbed, perhaps?"

"Or the next target." Barnes tossed a shirt to the far end of the table. "That's the last. No hidden gems. How'd it go at the university?"

"The professor, DeWijs, is busy, so I left the letters with him. We'll speak after the lecture tomorrow. Hopefully, the contents are more than talk of his family."

With nothing else about the murder or robberies uncovered, Hodgins headed home. He detoured to Fletcher's bookstore at Yonge and Shuter Streets to purchase an art book for Sara. When time permitted, she often sat on the front porch sketching the neighbours and passing buggies. With the aid of the clerk, he found one with both famous paintings and examples of how they were drawn.

After walking Scraps, he joined his eldest daughter in the backyard, playing with the twins.

"Sara, I have some homework for you." He held out the art book, wrapped with brown paper, tied with string.

"But Papa, it's summer. Teacher doesn't give us homework until September."

"Here." He waved the package.

Sara reluctantly took the book and removed the string. As the paper fell away, her eyes widened. "Oh, Papa!"

"I have tomorrow off. If your mother agrees, we can go to a lecture on art at the university. Someone's travelled all the way from Amsterdam University to lecture." He ruffled her hair. "And we've a special visitor coming to lunch."

* * *

With Hodgins' help, the chores, which usually took most of the day, were done well before their young guest arrived. Hodgins appraised the freshly cleaned house, shaking his head. "Delia, it's only Billy coming over. He won't expect every single bit of dust to be gone. The city's grimy enough that a new layer lands as soon as you finish dusting. Sit. Take a breath." He glanced up. "And take a minute to fix your hair."

"What?" Delia's hands flew up to her hairdo. Quite a few strands had worked their way out of the pins. Knuckles rapped on the front door, sending her flying upstairs to put herself back together.

The detective chuckled as he opened the door, pushing the dog aside. "Welcome, Billy. Don't mind the beast. Sorry, but our visit will have to be short as we're going to a lecture this afternoon. We have time for a good chat and lunch, though."

Sara peeked down the hall from the kitchen, observing the boy her father had often spoken of. Old enough to be her big brother, but not fully an adult. She came out with the twins. "Hello. I'm Sara. These are Holly and Ivy." The twins hid behind her skirt, still shy of strangers.

"Why don't we go into the sitting room? Sara, will you bring a tray with lemonade and glasses for everyone? Your mother will be down in a minute."

Sara returned as fast as she dared, making certain not to spill anything. She passed out the glasses and filled them, then sat beside Billy on the rosewood sofa, mesmerized as he told his stories of street life. The twins sat under the bay window with Scraps, the stranger in the room already forgotten. Delia joined them ten minutes later, hair fixed and dress changed.

"I've brought my sewing basket. Bertie said you need your jacket tailored. Stand up and let me see."

Billy stood as instructed, continuing his tales of street life while Delia pinned and sewed. She stood back to examine her work.

"There. Now you look like a proper gentleman. Remember, any time you get a new suit, if it doesn't fit properly, bring it here." The mantle clock chimed twelve. "Shall we retire to the dining room for lunch? I've got cold ham, vegetables, and biscuits made fresh this morning. And chocolate cake for dessert. Sara, you settle the twins, and I'll place the meal on the table.

Talk turned to Billy's new home and job, despite Sara asking questions about living day to day without a permanent home.

"You live all on your own?" Sara couldn't help asking. "Don't you have parents? Isn't it scary all by yourself?"

"Nah. Bin on me own for years. Got lots of friends." One by one, he answered Sara's questions, despite Delia continually admonishing her boldness.

After lunch, Delia and Sara washed up the dishes and put the leftover ham in the cold box. Billy walked with Hodgins to leave the twins next door with the Holloways, Henry Barnes' in-laws. They'd agreed to mind them until after he returned from the university.

Billy doffed his cap before Hodgins went up the Halloway's walk. "Thanks for the meal, detective. Can't recall the last time I sat down with a family." He went on his way, hands in pockets, whistling.

After changing into a dress more suitable for the summer heat, Delia and Sara joined Hodgins in the carriage he'd hired and headed to the university to listen to DeWijs' lecture.

* * *

Hodgins didn't pay much attention to the speaker. Instead, unanswered questions about the two murders occupied his thoughts. He looked around the lecture hall, amazed at the number of people attending. Cordelia nudged him and nodded at their daughter. Sara sat at the edge of the chair, listening with rapture. He smiled, glad she found it interesting. *Money well spent.*

Once the lecture ended and any questions answered, the detective and his family headed in the opposite direction from the crowd. DeWijs waited backstage for them. The professor smiled at Sara. "Did you enjoy my lecture, *kleintje?*"

Sara looked confused. "Pardon? Kli… what?"

"Little one. Do you have any questions?"

Sara opened her reticule and pulled out a folded paper. "Is this any good? Mommy's psychic friend said I'd be a painter when I grow up."

The professor took it and unfolded it. "I'm sure it is *prachtig*. Vonderful." He held the drawing of a horse and carriage over his leg and smoothed the wrinkles with his hand. "*Ja*, very nice. The carriage has much detail." He smiled at Sara. "The horse… maybe a little more practice? *Ja?*"

They spent almost a half hour discussing Sara's apparent talent before Hodgins reminded the professor why he came to the lecture.

"*Ja*. The letters." DeWijs removed the envelopes from his suit jacket pocket. "Two are personal, from his sister. I suppose you hoped to hear something of a crime? *Ja?*"

"Yes, unfortunately. Always think the worst in my job."

DeWijs smiled. "Then I will not disappoint you. The writer of the last letter mentions Dekker, the man the letter is addressed to, is to meet Mr. Jorginsen. There is talk of precious gems and a third man, unnamed."

"A third man? Interesting. No mention of places or dates?"

"*Nee*, nothing." He handed the letters, along with their translations, to Hodgins. "I am sorry to provide such little information."

"Not at all. You've proven that Dekker and Jorginsen knew each other, intentionally lodging at the same place to meet. You've also confirmed at least one other person is involved. Won't keep you any longer. Thank you for your assistance."

"Thank you, Professor DeWijs. I enjoyed listening to your lecture." Sara curtsied.

"It was a pleasure to meet you and your lovely mother."

As they exited the building, a gentle breeze blew, rustling through the trees. Since the heat had subsided somewhat, they walked to the Grand Opera Restaurant on Adelaide Street for dinner before going home to pick up the twins. The Halloways were always more than happy to help practice for when Violet gave them a grandchild.

* * *

The next day Hodgins returned to work, but not until he lingered at home late enough to see the family off to church. Barnes sat at his desk going over notes when the detective arrived. "Morning, Henry. When are you and Violet going to have a baby? Practically had to kidnap my girls from your in-laws."

"Working on it." Henry grinned. "Violet's mother has already started knitting baby things."

Hodgins perched on the corner of Henry's desk. "Got a translation of the letters found at Dekker's." He handed the English translation of the pertinent one to the constable. "There's a third person, unfortunately, he's not named."

Barnes scanned the letter. "A fence, possibly?"

"Possibly. Or a buyer. May even be the killer. Wonder if it would be worthwhile sending a letter to the Dutch police. Maybe they'll recognize the names."

"Might have it solved by the time an answer comes. You could ask that professor to deliver it."

"Since two of the letters are from Dekker's sister, she'll have to be informed. Better to come from the Korps Rijksveldwacht than a letter from me, delivered by a stranger."

"The Korps what, sir?"

"Amsterdam's National Police. Already looked them up, as we'll have to inform them of the deaths of Dekker and Jorginsen. May as well have a look around the United Empire Club. One of the members may have seen something."

CHAPTER SIXTEEN

Hodgins flagged down a hansom cab, then he and Barnes made their way to the club, located on the north side of King Street, between Bay and York. Neither of them knew much about it, as it had been open for less than a year. When they stepped out of the hansom, Hodgins walked up and down in front of the building, Barnes close behind.

"Quite impressive, sir. Why would a gentlemen's club need three-stories?"

"Suppose they wanted to make the members feel as though their membership money was well spent. Maybe the upper floor acts as a bordello. I hear it costs twenty dollars for the year. Those with money do like to show off. They listed the committee members in the newspaper when it opened. I recall Sir John A. Macdonald listed as a trustee. Do the notes say exactly where on the property Dekker's body was found?" Hodgins walked up a narrow lane on the west side of the Empire Club.

Barnes followed and took out his notebook to flip through the pages. He quickly found where he'd copied the notes from Roe. "Yes. He indicated Dekker was found on the east side, near the back wall."

The detective pointed. "There. Looks like a gate into the back." He walked over and reached out. "And it's not locked." They entered the yard and looked around. "Don't see any signs of a struggle. Maybe he was killed elsewhere and dumped here."

"Will we need to interview the members?" Barnes gulped. "Including the former prime minister?"

"I don't think we'll have to bother Macdonald, but we will have to speak with anyone who was at the club last Thursday. Someone must have seen or heard something unusual."

"You out there. This is private property. Off with you." A man Hodgins guessed to be in his thirties hollered at them through a window.

"Police, sir. We're investigating the death of a man found here a few days ago." Hodgins showed his badge. "Detective Hodgins. A word?"

Without replying, the window closed. A moment later, the man opened the back door and waved them in. Hodgins noticed his attire was not that of a caretaker. "Hurry. Don't want word getting out."

"Word's already out, sir. Didn't you see *The Globe?* Rather long write-up." Barnes still had his notebook out and flipped to a blank page. "Your name?"

The gentleman's eyes widened. "You're not going to print my name in the newspaper? That will never do."

"No, but we need to know who we're speaking with." Hodgins stood closer, towering over him, intentionally trying to intimidate. "My constable asked for your name."

"Campbell. Charles Campbell." A bead of sweat appeared on his forehead. "Club treasurer."

Campbell grew more nervous, fidgeting, and looking around.

Hodgins took another step closer. "Were you aware someone was found murdered on club property?

Campbell nodded. "Yes." He lowered his voice. "I spotted him. Sent one of the street lads for the police. Told him to send them around back. Locked the doors and went home."

Barnes' left eyebrow shot up. "You didn't stay and speak with the constable? I thought Constable Roe just forgot to write your name."

"Didn't want to get involved. Figured whoever came would look around and find him, and he did."

The detective shook his head and sighed. "Is there any way to find out who came to the club Thursday? We'll need to speak to each of them."

"No, that won't do. This is a private club, and member privacy must be respected."

"This is a murder investigation. I don't bloody care about their privacy. If you don't cooperate, I'll have to arrest you for interfering with my investigation."

"I'll have to speak with the committee first." Campbell wrung his hands. "Might take a few days."

"Well, get on with it. I expect all the names on my desk tomorrow, no later. Station House Four, Wilton Ave." Hodgins poked Campbell in the chest. "Tomorrow."

The detective turned and opened the back door, hesitating before exiting. He called over his shoulder. "By noon."

Barnes snapped his notebook closed and followed, hurrying to catch up to the long-legged detective. "Sir, do you think one of the members murdered this Dekker fellow, and possibly Jorginsen, too?"

"Who knows? Just because someone belongs to a fancy club doesn't mean they aren't capable of murder. It's possible one of them at least knows him. They could afford to buy the gems we found. We need to go over both Dekker's and Jorginsen's belongings again."

The detective hailed a passing cabriolet to take them back to the station house. Hodgins pondered deep in thought, so Barnes went over his notes, trying to figure out what they must have missed.

When they arrived, Hodgins helped Barnes bring everything out of the room where they stored the evidence, into one of the interrogation rooms.

"You go through Dekker's belongings, Henry. I'll go over Jorginsen's. There has to be something we missed."

"Harrington and I went through every piece of clothing, and examined every scrap of paper. I can't believe we missed something." Barnes set the suitcase at the opposite end of the table and opened it. One by one, he removed everything from inside. As he went to close the case, he bumped it, sending it to the floor. "Sir!"

Hodgins glanced over. "Find something?"

"The suitcase broke. There's a hidden compartment." Barnes reached into the gap, ripping more of the lining away. "A small book. Must be important."

Hodgins abandoned the search of Dekker's things and walked over to Barnes, taking the book. "Looks like a ledger." He flipped through the pages. "Appears to be a listing of transactions, but in some sort of code. I've seen it somewhere. Give me a minute." The detective searched his memory, then snapped his fingers. "It's the pigpen cipher. Been around 'bout three hundred years." He clapped Barnes on the back. "Good work. Sometimes it pays to be clumsy. I'll see if I can find the code to transcribe it." He put the book down and returned to Dekker's bag, dumping the contents on the floor. "Fetch me some scissors, will you?"

Barnes hurried to his desk and returned in less than a minute, scissors in hand. "Here. Do you think you might find something in the lining of the satchel, too?"

"Only one way to find out. It's not like he'll be needing to use this again." Hodgins took the scissors and cut the lining near the top large enough to get several fingers in, then ripped it the rest of the way.

"Shame. It was a nice, sturdy bag. Anything?"

"Give me a chance, Henry." He pulled the lining down to the bottom, and several sheets of stationery fell out. "Hmm. A list of ships, ports, dates, and times."

"Smugglers? I haven't heard about any gem smuggling, have you?" Barnes peered over the detective's shoulder to read the notes.

"No, nothing. Could be something new. Look." Hodgins pointed to the top two lines. "Only two of these dates are in the past, and one of the ships came from Rotterdam. There's a new route for ships. Just a few years ago they opened up the *Nieuwe Waterweg*, almost thirteen miles long. It was designed to connect the North Sea with the Rhine and Meuse Rivers in order to reach inland as far as Switzerland and France."

"You've lost me, sir. *Nieuwe* sounds like new. *Waterweg* must have something to do with water. A new canal? How do you know all this?"

"I read, Henry. And yes, you figured out the basic translation. Trade with the Netherlands has expanded, and Rotterdam has been an important port since, oh, mid to late fifteen hundreds. They have to continue to expand, or a trade route will open somewhere else."

The constable read the date of the first ship. "Sir, Jorginsen's been here about a week, correct?"

"Assuming he rented the room at the boarding house when he arrived, yes."

"He must have come over on this ship." He pointed to the second one on the list. "It arrived in Toronto July twenty-third. Less than two weeks before his body was found."

Hodgins fiddled with his moustache, re-curling the waxed ends that drooped in the August heat. "You're right.

He must have left the gems sewn into his suit until he found a better hiding place. Or until the buyer arrived."

"So, not a local robbery. Do you think Dekker's body was left behind the United Empire Club for a reason? Could the buyer be one of the members?"

Hodgins whistled. "I hope not. Most of them are likely prominent businessmen and politicians. We'll just have to wait for Campbell to bring the list tomorrow. Meanwhile, we'll have to keep an eye out for the rest of the ships on this list. Write out a couple of copies and pass them along to Harrington and Riddell."

"Right away. Shall I go back to the boarding house and ask if anyone spoke to either man or saw them with other people? They must have had contact with someone in the city."

"Good idea. You do that after you write out the lists. I think I'll read the translations of the other two letters. DeWijs said they were personal from Dekker's sister. Maybe there's a clue in one of them."

The detective headed to his office, leaving the mess in the interrogation room for later. He pulled the letters out of his desk drawer and began to read. Mostly talk of the family and a new baby being born while he was in Canada.

"What?" He re-read the paragraph again, slammed his palm on the desktop and shouted, "Eureka!"

He flipped his notebook to the last page of notes and made additions before calling for Barnes. "Henry, a connection. Get one of the lads to copy out the shipping list and get in here."

Barnes dropped the original and half-copied lists on Harrington's desk before hurrying into the detective's office. "What have you found?"

"Wish I'd read those translations as soon as DeWijs gave them to me. Never underestimate what personal letters will reveal." He handed one of the translations to the constable. "Read this. Skip to the fourth paragraph."

Barnes took the page and counted down. His mouth opened as he read, a grin creeping across his face. "Can it be this easy?"

"Probably not, but one can hope. She didn't say if this Hendrik person is a friend or family, but he's living in the hamlet of Lemonville. Find it on a map, will you, Henry? I think I need to plan a trip."

CHAPTER SEVENTEEN

When Hodgins arrived home that evening, he sat in the kitchen while Delia prepared dinner, letting her know he'd be out on another train adventure again in the morning. "Do you have anything I can take to eat on the train? You know how I hate the sandwiches they sell on board."

"I'm sure I can find something. So, tell me. Where are you off to, and for how long? Another early train and late return?"

"Up to Aurora. Actually, I'll be visiting the little hamlet of Lemonville. I have a few options for the train north. First train will get me there early and allow time to hire a horse to get to Lemonville. Not looking forward to catching the 7:37 train, but I don't know what I'll run into once there. At least it won't require staying overnight. The last train gets me back in Toronto just before nine-thirty this evening, but I hope to catch one of the earlier ones. Just need to track someone down and inform him of a death. Give me a chance to find out if he's involved in the murders and thefts, or just an acquaintance of the deceased. At the very least, he can inform the family back in Amsterdam."

"I'm glad it's not overnight. I hate it immensely when you're not here at night. So, where is this little hamlet? Is it far from Aurora?"

"It's southeast, about nine or ten miles. Will be a quicker ride without a rig, and it's looking like tomorrow will be as nice as today. Haven't ridden for some time. Hope I don't get thrown."

"Ask for Buttercup. They always have one with a name like that, for the ladies." Cordelia grinned and began chopping up carrots.

"Not funny, but you may be closer to the truth than you think. I've gotten soft in my old age. Once this case is closed, how about we take the family riding? Must be some place around with a pony for Sara since she's only ridden one time. The twins will have to ride with us. I'll check with Mitchell. I know he has a pony."

Cordelia continued with the meal preparation. Curious about her husband's trip the next day, she asked for more information. "Tell me about this person you're visiting. Why is he important?"

"All I know is his name is Hendrik Van Dijk, and he was mentioned in a letter from Dekker's sister."

"Oh, one of the letters the art professor translated?"

"Yes. This sister, Annika, asked if Dekker had been to Lemonville to visit, and to send her warmest regards. Could be an accomplice, family friend, a cousin—"

"Or she's sweet on him." Cordelia stopped slicing the last of the cold ham and turned to face him. "I'll bet you never thought of that, did you?"

Hodgins leaned back in the chair, surprised. "How did you ever come up with that conclusion? She only mentioned him in one sentence."

"Warmest regards. She didn't ask her brother to simply say hello, but to send her *warmest* regards. And why mention Hendrik at all? If he was family, she'd have written a letter directly to Hendrik."

"I'll ask him, shall I? Good morning, Hendrik. Can you tell me if you have a sweetheart back home named Annika Dekker?"

Cordelia threw a piece of cut carrot at him. "Go fetch the girls and get them ready for dinner."

* * *

Overnight, the cooling breeze had moved on, making it difficult for Hodgins to sleep. He rose early, careful not to wake his wife. He dressed and took Scraps for an early morning walk. The neighbourhood remained peaceful, waiting for the darkness to lift. Not even the birds were up. They walked for almost an hour, the dog sniffing and exploring everything, the detective thinking about the murders and stolen gems.

He'd left instructions with Barnes to split up the list of United Empire Club members between himself, Riddell, and Harrington. Hodgins suggested having the new constable, Jones, assist, since Riddell wasn't able to walk long distances due to the injury received the previous year.

For the time being, they'd leave former Prime Minister Macdonald out of the investigation.

When Hodgins and Scraps finally got back to the house, everyone still slept. He gave Scraps a few pieces of ham, then sliced off some bread and made a sandwich for the trip. The dog trotted upstairs while Hodgins wrote out a note for Delia, then slipped out to begin the walk to Union Station. Along with the birds, the trolley and cabriolet drivers were nowhere to be seen. Hodgins stopped along the way to purchase the early edition of *The Globe* to read on the train.

He skimmed the front page, shaking his head as he read of the wreck of the Steamer Mersey. The captain and fourteen men lost. Hodgins muttered over the article about the hanging in England of Mr. Fish for the murder of a seven-year-old girl. "Good riddance."

Page three announced the posting of the voters list for the upcoming Legislative Assembly election. With nothing else of much interest on the four pages of the paper, he settled back and read the long article on The Queen's Cup.

Finally, the train pulled into the Aurora station. As he exited, he noticed the temperature had risen without the slight breeze from Lake Ontario reaching so far north. Hodgins fanned his face with his homburg as he walked into town to hire a horse for the day. It didn't take long to locate the livery run by David McLeod. He negotiated a fair price for the use of a single horse, no buggy.

Hodgins mounted the chestnut bay and stroked its neck. "You'd better be good-natured, boy. Take it nice and easy with me, but not too slow." He flicked the reins and began his journey. First, down Yonge Street, then across the second concession he came to, and across that to concession seven. Turing south brought him to the tiny hamlet an hour after starting.

The first building he approached was the Lemonville Methodist Church. He halted the horse in front, dismounted, and walked over to a person tending one of the graves. "Excuse me. I'm looking for someone and wondered if you could help. His name is Hendrik Van Dijk. You wouldn't know him, would you?"

"Might. Who are you, if you don't mind me asking?" Hodgins guessed the man to be in his fifties, with the appearance of someone not unfamiliar with hard work. Hodgins noticed the calloused hands and skin darkened by many hours in the sun. *Caretaker?*

"My name is Albert Hodgins, detective with the Toronto Constabulary. I have news for him that's best given in person."

"Death, then?"

Hodgins nodded.

"Two farms down, on the left. Hired hand, keeps to himself." The man turned away and went back to pulling weeds around the graves.

"Thank you." Hodgins sighed and rubbed his sore behind before mounting the horse and trotting down the dirt road, turning up the second laneway. Several people worked in the fields, but he continued to the house. When he knocked on the door, a young girl around sixteen answered.

"May I help you? Daddy's not home, but he's not hiring help right now."

"Good afternoon, miss. I'm not looking for work. I need to speak with one of your hired hands. Mr. Van Dijk."

"Who's at the door, Emma?" A woman in her late thirties came down the hall, wiping her hands with her apron.

"Man looking for Hendrik."

"I'll speak with him. Go back to the kitchen and finish up." She turned to Hodgins. "You're looking for Hendrik? May I inquire why?"

"Delicate matter." He introduced himself. "I need to inform him of a death. May I speak with him?"

"Gracious. A family member?"

Hodgins shrugged. "Don't rightly know. His name was mentioned in a letter found at the deceased's home. We've no one to translate a letter to the family into Dutch. Thought Mr. Van Dijk could inform the family in their native tongue. It would be more personal than a letter from the police."

"I see. He should be tending to the horses. We've one who bred late, and he's keeping watch in case the birth is difficult again." She stepped out onto the porch and pointed. "That barn over there."

"Thank you, ma'am. Won't keep him long."

Hodgins left his mount drinking from a trough in front of the house and walked to the barn. "Mr. Van Dijk?"

"Here." A head popped up over the boards of a stall.

"Mr. Van Dijk, I'm Detective Hodgins. I believe you know Hans Dekker."

"*Ja.* Hans is good friend."

"I'm sorry to tell you, he's been found dead. Murdered."

Van Dijk reached for the top of the stall to steady himself. "Murdered? Why would anyone murder Hansy?"

"We're looking into that. We found your name in a letter from his sister. We have the return address, but no one at the station speaks Dutch. The person who translated for us has already returned to Amsterdam. Would you be able to send a letter to let them know?"

"*Ja, ja.* I will tell Annika. Their parents are dead. She has no one else."

Annika, not Miss. Dekker. Cordelia might be right. "Maybe write a friend who could relay the news to Miss. Dekker? Best she not be alone when she finds out. Could you tell me what business Dekker was in? We're having trouble figuring out what brought him to Toronto."

"He worked on ships with his friend Willehelm Jorginsen. Neither speak much English. Does he know?"

"Well, he's, um, also been murdered. His family will also need to be informed."

Van Dijk blew out a breath. "*Mijn woord.* Why?"

"I'm afraid we don't know. Is there anyone in the city either man would have contacted?"

Van Dijk shook his head. "Maybe. He say money coming, but not say from where. Was meeting man this week."

"And you don't know his name?"

The Dutchman shook his head. "*Nee.*"

Both men turned their heads when the horse let out a loud whinny. "Must go. I think is time."

Hodgins peered over into the stall at the horse, now lying on its side. "Good luck."

He went back to fetch the Belgian and began the long trek back to Aurora. After returning the horse, Hodgins barely had enough time to get to the train station and purchase his ticket back to Union Station.

CHAPTER EIGHTEEN

Once settled on the train, Hodgins took out his hanky and wiped his face. The previously clean, white linen turned a nasty shade of dark grey. Tired from a restless night and riding the horse between Aurora and Lemonville in the sun, he fell asleep before the train left the station. Fortunately, the porter recognized him from numerous other trips and woke him as they approached Union Station in Toronto.

The detective went straight for the kettle when he arrived at the police station. Despite the heat, a hot cup of tea was a welcome liquid for his dry throat. He carried his teacup, hoping to speak with Constable Barnes, but found his desk empty. Harrington and Jones were also absent.

"Riddell. Where is everyone?"

"Out working on that list of Empire members. I did as much as I could, but ..." He patted his leg. "Jonesy took the rest of my portion." He heaved a mournful sigh. "I'm useless."

"None of that, Tom. You're lucky your eye and ankle healed. After the beating that crook gave you, you could have been left half-blind and unable to use that leg at all. Don't ever think you're useless." Hodgins clapped Tom on the back. "Even a blind squirrel finds a nut once in a while. You've taken well to the photographic equipment, and no, Jones will not be replacing you. He's a backup for when you're busy or off work. You've a sharp mind, and we need that. He's got an in at one of the photographic studios. Get him to introduce you. That way, you can keep current with changes. They've come a long way since the camera obscura."

Riddell smiled. "Didn't know you knew about photography."

"Don't, really. Recall reading something about it once. For some reason, the name stuck in my brain."

"Wish someone would approve upgrading the equipment to something more modern. The glass plates we use are heavy. Dry plate negatives are much lighter."

"One day, I'm sure. It's not at the top of the police budget, unless you'd like a pay cut. Now, tell me about the people you interviewed."

"The ones I spoke to were either out of town, sick, or had alibis. Still have to confirm they were where they said, but I got no sense of lies from any of them. How was your trip to Limetown?"

Hodgins laughed. "Lemonville. Van Dijk seemed genuinely surprised when I told him Dekker was dead. He mentioned Dekker told him he was expecting to come into money, but didn't know how. Just that he was to meet a man. Also said Dekker and Jorginsen worked on ships. Easy way to smuggle goods. He did say he'd write to a friend to relay the news to Dekker's sister and Jorginsen's family. One less thing for us to do."

Hodgins drank the last of his tea, then headed to the back for a refill before going into his office. He flipped through his notes, trying to decide the best way to continue. He turned to a blank page in his notebook, scribbling as he thought. *Back to the boarding house to see if either man had other visitors.* He tapped his pencil against his chin. *Who else? How can I find the mystery man?* Frustrated, he tossed his pencil down and slammed his notebook closed.

He checked his pocket watch. *By the time I get to the boarding house, Thompson will likely be sitting down for his evening meal. Won't be in a good mood if I interrupt.* He got up and went over to Riddell. "I'm heading home. If any of the constables find something that requires immediate attention, send them 'round. I'll be heading to the boarding house on King before coming in tomorrow."

* * *

Hodgins enjoyed a leisurely breakfast with his family. He wanted to ensure Mr. Thomson's belly would be full when he arrived. "It's not often we get to do this. I'm either rushing off to work or to catch a train, and Sara is out the door for school."

Cordelia placed a portion of scrambled eggs on everyone's plate. "And on your days off, you're usually fast asleep until noon."

"Slight exaggeration, but yes. I do like my sleep when I can get it. Another few years and the twins will be off to school as well."

"How was your trip yesterday? You were too tired to talk last night."

He sighed. "Not as useful as I thought. I don't believe Van Dijk is involved, and the only clue he gave me wasn't really helpful. There seems to be another man involved, but that's all he knew." Hodgins sliced off a thick piece of freshly baked bread and smothered it in homemade apple jelly.

After devouring half of the bread and most of the eggs, he reached for his tea. "Marvellous, as always. I wish I had some idea who this man could be. How in tarnation can I know where to look when I don't know anything about this man or the meeting? Where was it supposed to take place? When? 'This week' is all Van Dijk said. There's over eighty thousand people in the city. Could be any one of them. Or a visitor."

"You'll find him, Papa. You always do." Sara smiled at her father. "Right, Mama?"

"Yes, Sara. He always does."

Hodgins ruffled Sara's hair. "I'm glad you have such faith in me. I'll do my best."

"No luck at the distillery or the Empire Club?" Delia began to clear the dishes.

"No. I'll get an update from the lads when I get to the station. Since no one came looking for me last night, it doesn't seem like they had any luck. I'm going to the boarding house to see if anyone shows up looking for either Dekker or Jorginsen."

"What about the jewels, Papa?"

"Haven't found them yet. Have to be somewhere." He thought for a moment. "I wonder. Could there be a hiding place at the boarding house in Dekker's room? Why didn't I think of that earlier? He was identified as the robber at the first jewellery store a few days after the charwoman found Jorginsen's body. No idea if he was the robber at the second jeweller's. Either he stashed the gems somewhere, or he already met with the mystery man. Hands over the goods and gets murdered instead of paid?"

"But if he was to meet someone this week, is it possible that man killed him? He wouldn't be showing up at the boarding house if he did." Cordelia refilled his teacup.

"And he was found dead the same day as the second robbery, which means he was likely killed before the robbery. There has to be another thief. I completely forgot to ask how long he'd been dead. Stonehouse left the report on my desk, and I haven't even read it." He gulped down the last of his tea and left the table. "I need to read that before I go to the boarding house. Sara, you'll have to walk Scraps."

Hodgins raced out of the house as he shrugged into his suit jacket. Despite the heat, he ran until he found an empty cabriolet to take him the rest of the way to the station. None of the constables he was working with had arrived yet. He found the coroner's report on his desk and skimmed it for the approximate time of death. Six to eight hours. *After the robbery*. Not sure if Thompson would be up and fed, he took his time walking to the boarding house. Forty-five minutes later, Abby led him to the sitting room.

"He's just finishing up. Shall I let him know you're here, or wait till he's done eating?"

"Wait, I think. Don't want to spoil his meal. Maybe you can help if you've got a minute?"

Abby sat in the chair opposite. "How?"

"Has anyone come in recently looking for either Dekker or Jorginsen?"

"Nah. Jest you and the other coppers."

"Would the landlord know if any visitors came?"

Abby laughed. "He don't get involved much with the lodgers except to take their money."

"Okay, good. I'll still ask him, but can you do me a favour?"

The char girl scooched to the edge of the chair, nodding.

"If anyone comes looking for them, don't say they're dead. Just say they've gone out, and get the man's name. When you've some free time, come tell me, or find a constable and tell him. Can you do that?"

"Oh, sure. That's easy." She frowned. "What if he comes on my day off?"

"Who answers the door when you're not here? Mr. Thompson?"

"No. One of the lodgers, if they notice. Can't always hear someone knocking from upstairs. Tol' Mr. Thompson to get one of them crank ringers, but he won't."

"Yes, they are handy. Have one myself. If I don't hear from you in a few days, I'll come back and see if anyone else saw him. Maybe he already heard, and won't be coming."

"Abby!"

"Uh-oh. I'd better scarper. I'll tell him you're waiting."

Thompson made the detective wait another five minutes before joining him in the sitting room. Hodgins only needed a few minutes with the landlord as he confirmed what Abby said. He couldn't be bothered to answer the door, as that apparently was "the girl's job."

On the way back to the Station House, Hodgins stopped at Morrison's. He browsed the jewellery while he waited for Morrison to finish with a customer. *Wonder how much custom jewellery costs? Sara's old enough for a nice pendant.*

"Help you with something, Detective? Found my stolen gems yet?"

"Afraid not. Do you have any pendants suitable for a twelve-year-old girl? For my daughter's birthday in January."

"That's five months away. Why are you really here?"

"Just wanted to update you and Cobb on the thefts. I noticed his window is still boarded up. You mentioned hiring night security. Have you done that?"

"Yes. Myself, Cobb and two other jewellers on the street chipped in. He's been on duty since Saturday."

"Has he seen anyone suspicious?"

"Just the usual hooligans and drunks. No one has tried to break in. Have you caught the guy?"

Hodgins shook his head. "We believe we know who broke into both stores, but unfortunately, he's been killed. We have a lead on a partner." *A very vague lead.* "Remember, if you or your hired security see anything, you're to report it immediately. If a gang is involved, they'll be dangerous. We've increased the frequency our constable is patrolling this area, and added a few more until the culprit is caught. If you find him, don't anything stupid. I'm going to check in on Cobb. Tell the other two what I just said."

After speaking with Mr. Cobb, the detective went back to the station to try to figure out his next steps. *Who is this other person Dekker had a meeting with? A fence? Buyer? Partner in crime?*

One by one, the constables returned from interviewing the last few members of the United Empire Club. They'd been able to locate most the day before, but had the same results as Riddell. Many had alibis that were easily checked. Barnes, being the senior constable, gathered everyone's notebooks and joined Hodgins in his office.

"We've several alibis to confirm, but they all appear to be innocent of the murders. One of the men on my list was at the club that night, but he left shortly before the alarm was raised." Barnes flipped to the page with that interview. "Some of the men gathered for several rounds of Whist. They were there for several hours. Harrington interviewed a few of the other players, and they all said the same."

Hodgins leaned back. "Sounds like it may have been where a chase ended rather than a meet-up. Dekker must have run up the alley thinking he could get away. Hid behind the building, was found, then bludgeoned to death. Do any of the members have any connection to jewellery?"

"I don't believe so. None that I spoke to, and none of the other lads mentioned it."

"Hmm. That slip of paper with ship names, when's the next one due in, I wonder?" Hodgins flipped through the file he'd started and pulled out the torn page. "Here. Not for a few days yet. Coming in from India. Wonder if it's continuing on to New York from here. Another good port for smugglers. Give the lads back their books and each of you write out the names and professions on a separate sheet of paper. Maybe something will fall into place. This afternoon, confirm the rest of the alibis, if you can. I'll have a chat with the constable called to the scene." He flipped back through his notes. "Roe. See what he can recall of the sight."

"He's on the evening shift."

"Guess I'll be missing my supper."

With no leads to follow, Hodgins went back to both crime scenes. The alley by the distillery had been somewhat cleaned up. *Wind must have blown the trash onto another property.* He walked the length of it, trying to see if there were any other ways in. The area around the building was fenced off, creating a dead end, so he turned back and headed up Parliament Street to King and hailed a cab to take him over to the United Empire Club.

As he snooped around the area where the body was found, he noticed a face at a back window. Campbell. The detective waved, but the face disappeared. He waited, but no one came out the back door. *No one enjoys speaking to the constabulary.* He chuckled and continued searching. Any blood loss would have long since soaked into the ground, but the grass was trampled in one area. *Must be where he was found.* The property was well kept, and any possible clues would have vanished once the body had been removed.

Finding nothing further at either location, he walked back to the station. With over an hour left before Roe would come in for his shift, Hodgins took his time.

CHAPTER NINETEEN

Hodgins paced around his office while waiting for Constable Roe to come in. Eventually, he ended up in the outer office, where all the constables sat. Several gave him funny looks and shifted nervously in their chairs. A few whispered. Realizing he made them uncomfortable, the detective went out into the heat for a walk. The sun began its slow descent, but still remained well above the horizon. After making a dozen trips around the block, he sat on the entrance steps to wait.

Bit by bit, the constables came in to write up reports before the end of shift. He'd asked several if they were Roe before someone gave him a description.

"Roe? He's a lazy one. Takes his time to do everything. Can't say I've ever seen anyone walk so slow. Fancies himself a bit of a dandy. Usually comes in late for his shift. You'll know 'im when ya see 'im."

A few minutes later, he spotted the man. Took ten minutes to walk the short distance from Parliament. Anyone else would have covered the distance in no more than two minutes. Roe walked with a saunter, head held at an angle of superiority, a smug look on his face.

Hodgins stood. "Roe? A word."

Roe nodded.

"Today, if you don't mind."

"Certainly." Roe sped up from sloth to snail.

"How did you get hired as a member of the constabulary? Have you ever had to give chase?"

Roe raised his eyebrows in surprise. "Chase? Why would I do that?"

"Maybe to catch a crook? Never mind. I need to speak with you about that body you found behind the United Empire Club. My office."

The detective turned and went straight to his office, then stood at the doorway watching Roe saunter across the room, nodding and waving to everyone in sight.

"Roe!"

The desk sergeant hurried past Roe to speak with Hodgins. "He's a cousin to the Chief. Tread carefully."

"Don't bloody care. He's not fit to wear the uniform. Get him assigned to me and I'll take care of him. He'll be gone in less than a week."

Roe finally made it to Hodgins' office. He entered, sat in a chair in front of the desk, placing his feet on the edge of the desktop.

Hodgins swatted them off. "Sit up straight. Show at least a little respect for my rank. And wipe that smug grin off your face. Tell me everything you saw or found at the scene."

Roe took his notebook from his trousers pocket and tossed it towards Hodgins. "It's all in there."

The detective thumbed through it, not stopping until he reached the end of the notes. Less than two dozen pages filled. He looked up at Roe, then flipped the pages back again. The fourth to last page had only three sentences. Hodgins read them aloud. "Dead man behind United Empire Club, east side, by back wall. Head bashed in. No identification."

He tossed the book back. "That's it? That's all you wrote? My three-year-old twins could have done better. Did you actually look at the body? Check the area? Ask anyone in the vicinity questions?"

"I looked in his pockets. No one was around. Who would I ask? It was dark, so I couldn't see anything."

"Who would… Dark? Someone in a neighbouring building might have heard a fight and looked out a window. Maybe lent you a lantern. Did you even bother to go out the next day to look around? And don't tell me it's not your shift. You could have asked one of the lads. Left a note for someone to check the area first thing."

Roe shrugged. "Is that all, sir? I'd like to get ready. My shift is starting, after all."

"Get out of my office. You'd better hope you have some sort of skill, because I'm going to do my damnedest to make sure you never put that uniform on again."

"I'll give the chief your regards at dinner tomorrow." The smug look returned, along with a sly grin, as he sauntered out.

Hodgins threw his own notebook at the wall. "Don't care who you're having dinner with. I'll have a scathing report on his desk before I leave. Bloody incompetent, miserable, vazey ratbag."

Hodgins wrote out a lengthy report detailing Roe's incompetence and left it in the centre of the Chief's desk where he couldn't miss it. Feeling slightly better once getting that out of his system, he smiled and headed out.

As he approached the sergeant's desk, Cooper called out. "Are you certain you want to leave that, Detective? Maybe give it a day or two?"

"Nonsense. Roe's a disgrace to the uniform. The three sentences he wrote about Dekker's murder were the longest description of anything I saw in his notebook. Two dozen pages covered six months of incidents. Who knows how much evidence has been lost? I don't care who he's related to. He's hampered my murder investigation, and I want the Chief to know. Good evening, Cooper."

* * *

When Hodgins arrived at the station the next morning, he found a note on his desk. After reading it, he took a deep breath. *Wonder what rank I'll have five minutes from now? If I even have a job.* He took the note with him to the chief's office and waved it. "You wanted to see me, sir?"

The Chief tapped the lengthy note Hodgins left the night before. "This is quite the report, Detective. Maybe you were a little out of sorts when you wrote it?"

Hodgins stood in front of the chief's desk, head held high, shoulders back, waiting for his dismissal from the force. "No. Not out of sorts, sir. Angry. I realize Roe is your cousin, but he's the most incompetent person I've ever come across." He relaxed when the Chief nodded, and leaned forward, both hands on the back of the chair in front of the desk.

"You should see the notes he's written about the calls he's been on. Calling them notes is a stretch. He doesn't speak to anyone, no attempt to find witnesses, doesn't look for clues or evidence. If we have to rely on his note-taking in court, we'd never convict anyone."

"No one else has said one bad word against my cousin. Think they're all afraid to. You know, he's not even my blood. The wife's cousin's son. And you're right. He *is* a… what did you call him?" The chief re-read the note and chuckled. "A vazey ratbag. Totally agree. I'll see what I can do about him."

Hodgins stared, mouth agape.

"That's all. Go find your murderer."

"Yes, sir."

Surprised, Hodgins made his way back to his office, detouring to Barnes' desk. All the constables he'd given assignments to sat at their desks. "Up-date, boys?"

Riddell, Harrington, and Jones gathered around Barnes' desk. "So far, everyone's checked out. We've compiled a list of the United Empire Club members and their jobs. None of them seems to have any connection to jewellery or gemstones." Barnes smiled. "One of them has a brother working at a distillery. Wonder if he gets free samples?"

"If he does, they're probably smuggled out. Can't see any distillery allowing profits to go home with their employees. Which distillery?"

Barnes looked over the list. "Doesn't say. Jonesy, that was off your part of the list, wasn't it?"

"Yes. Didn't think it was important, so I didn't write it down. If I recall, it was Gooderham's."

"Gooderham's?" Hodgins and Barnes looked at each other.

"Is that important?" Jones looked worried. "Did I need to write that down?"

"Yes, but don't fret. You're still learning. Remember to make a note of everything you hear or find. It's often the most innocent of comments or the tiniest item that turns the case upside down. Jorginsen's body was found outside Gooderham and Worts. Could just be a coincidence, but then again…"

"It's a connection. Got it." Jones opened his notebook, flipped to the pages with interviews and added in Gooderham.

Before they could discuss it further, someone rushed into the station, hollering.

"I've been robbed."

All heads turned.

Don't let it be another jeweller. Hodgins walked over to the distraught man.

Cooper gestured towards Hodgins. "The detective here will help you."

"What seems to have been taken?

"A diamond. Ten carats. Worth hundreds of thousands of dollars."

"Come into my office." The detective called to Barnes. "Join us."

Once settled, Hodgins indicated for Barnes to take notes. "Let's start with your name and address."

"Fitzsimmons. George Fitzsimmons. My shop is at 8 King Street East. One of several businesses in the building." His eyes widened. "There's another jeweller downstairs. Didn't think to check with him. Welch is his name."

"We'll speak with him. You said a ten-carat diamond. Is that the only gem that was taken?"

"Only one taken? Isn't that enough? Worth more than your salary over the length of your career, I'm sure."

"Yes, probably. How did the thief gain access?"

"Busted my door. Must have known about the diamond, as nothing else was taken."

Barnes looked up from his notebook. "How many people knew about it?"

"Well, a few. Welch knows as he's been in to look at it. Don't get diamonds that size often. And my family. No one else. It just arrived a few days ago."

"Don't suppose any of your family is a member of the United Loyalist Club? Or maybe works at Gooderham and Worts?" Hodgins knew it was a long shot, but needed confirmation.

"Wife's nephew works at Gooderham's." Realization dawned on Fitzsimmons. "You're not accusing young

Theodore? Barely has the brains to grind the malt. He's only seventeen."

"Questions we have to ask, sir. I'm not accusing anyone, just getting all the information possible." Hodgins thought for a moment. "Could he have told anyone?"

Fitzsimmons blew out a breath. "Yes, that's very likely. That boy always shoots off his mouth without thinking. Don't imagine any of his acquaintances would be able to break into my safe. Bust the front door, yes."

"Is there anything else you can tell us?" Barnes sat, pencil poised.

"Only that it happened after 8:00 p.m. That's when I left. When I came in a half hour ago, the door was broken and the diamond gone."

"Barnes, have Riddell and Jones gather up the photography equipment and go to 8 King East. I'll flag down a carriage. Mr. Fitzsimmons, we'll come with you to your shop. Barnes can speak with Welch while I follow you."

CHAPTER TWENTY

The trip to 8 King Street East only took ten minutes. The detective headed upstairs with Fitzsimmons while Barnes went directly to Welch's business on the first floor to see if the owner noticed anything awry.

"I can see how it would have been quite a shock to find your door hanging on the hinges. If anyone had been in one of the nearby offices, they would have heard something. Show me where the diamond was kept."

Fitzsimmons led Hodgins into his office at the back and pointed. "There. I'd been trying to come up with a design for the setting. Instead of the safe, I put it in the cabinet behind my desk. I assure you it was locked. No one could have known it was there."

"You didn't mention it to anyone once you'd arrived home?"

The jeweller shook his head. "No. It's just myself and my wife. She enjoys the jewellery I make for her, but she has little interest in the goings-on of the business."

"No way your nephew could have found out?"

Fitzsimmons shook his head. "He wasn't there."

Hodgins examined the cabinet. "Very good quality. Excellent craftmanship." More than one drawer sat open. "I see just the one drawer has a lock. The thief must have been searching through the unlocked drawers first. No doubt you've heard of the other robberies on King West?"

Fitzsimmons nodded. "Morrison's been around."

The detective began talking to himself. "The first one had the safe blown. The second seems to have been less violent. The thief hid away until the shop was closed. Broke out rather than in. All the robberies appear to have been done by different people. Thieves generally use the same method, but I believe they're all connected. A leader, if you will, hiring different people to steal the items."

He turned his attention to the jeweller. "This one must have taken a chance that he'd find something of value in the cabinet. Checked the unlocked drawers as they were easiest to access, then the locked one. It's possible your safe may have been blown if the diamond hadn't been found. My constables should be here shortly to photograph the damage. Please don't move anything until they've finished."

"Detective?" Riddell and Jones entered the back office.

"Take pictures of the front door and the damage in here. When you're done, meet me at Welch's business on the first floor."

As he left Fitzsimmons', a couple of businessmen passed the broken door, giving it a curious stare. Hodgins nodded at them, then joined Barnes on the lower level. "Anything?"

"Didn't think so at first, but it does appear that someone tried to pick the door lock, then gave up. Strange, isn't it? Tried to pick this lock, but just busted the door upstairs?"

Hodgins knelt in front of the door, examining the lock. "Peculiar. Maybe the thief thought someone outside would hear. This business is very near the street entrance. No way to tell if he tried to get in when he first entered, or thought to give it a go on the way out. May not even have any connection to the other thefts. A simple lock hasn't prevented the other thieves. Nothing taken?"

Welsh listened to the exchange, arms crossed over his chest. "Doesn't appear he got in. Not so much as a pencil missing. If you're through, I'd like to get ready. My salesman will be arriving any time, and I need to open in a half hour." He uncrossed his arms and leaned closer. "Something stolen from Fitzy?"

"You'll have to take that up with him." Hodgins turned to Barnes. "Fetch another carriage, will you? Riddell and Jones should be about done."

The other two constables came down to Welsh's business just before Barnes returned. They all piled into the carriage and headed back to the station.

Fifteen minutes later, Barnes joined Hodgins in his office. "This is a strange case, sir. Two dead men, one with hidden gems, and three robberies. They all appear to be different, but they have to be connected."

"I was certain Dekker murdered Jorginsen, but he's dead, too. The note found in Dekker's suitcase indicates there may be a smuggling ring. We need to find out who's behind it. There must be rumours floating around. Might be time to get in touch with Billy again. Even though he's got a proper job, he still has his contacts. More, probably. The newspapers have their own informants." Hodgins pulled his pad of foolscap from his desk drawer. "Time to compile everything we know, and make a list of questions."

"Should we continue to look at the members of the United Empire Club? The only connection to anyone so far is Fitzsimon's nephew working at Gooderham and Worts."

"There's something that doesn't feel right about that. He's only seventeen-years-old, and to all accounts, not very bright. I still feel the club and distillery are connected somehow. I don't believe either Gooderham or Worts has anything to do with it. Haven't spoken to Worts yet as he's still out of town. Would be difficult for him to relay information quick enough if he was involved. Someone who works there, possibly. And I don't think it to be a coincidence Dekker's body ended up behind the club. Some sort of message, possibly? Have you finished checking the alibis?"

Barnes pulled a folded paper from his notebook. "I still have a few to track down. Harrington, Riddell, and Jones have crossed all their names off."

"See if you can find them. I'll make my list, then try to find Billy. Doubt he'll be at the newspaper office, so it may take a while."

Hodgins spent over a half hour going through his notebook and transferring details from his inquires, as well as what he'd added from the constables, onto one sheet. He underlined the United Empire Club and Gooderham and Worts Distillery, placing a question mark after each. Then he circled the three robbery locations. As he read through the list, he paused at Van Dijk. *Could he know more than he let on? Another trip is needed.*

He folded the large sheet of foolscap and tucked it between the pages of his notebook, then headed out to find Billy. As expected, the lad wasn't at the newspaper office. Hodgins walked around the area the former street urchin previously haunted. Finally, as the afternoon wore on, he went to the boarding house on Bond Street where the boy now resided.

The landlady opened the door, letting the aroma of an apple pie drift out. "I remember you. Police friend of Billy. Lad ain't here. Left early and didn't say when he'd return. Sorry."

"I didn't really think he'd be home. He's most likely out digging up information for a story. Couldn't find him at any of his usual spots." The detective tipped his homburg. "Thank you for your time." Before he had a chance to turn, a voice called out.

"Detective. Ya lookin' fer me?"

"Billy! I'm hoping you've still got your ear to the wind. Maybe heard something that will help me. Have time for a chat?"

"Certainly. Come 'round the back and we can sit in the garden." Billy came up the walk and placed his arm around the landlady's shoulders. "Maybe Mrs. Nelson has some of that iced tea that's becoming popular."

The detective made a face. "Haven't tried that yet. Can't imagine drinking cold tea on purpose."

Billy laughed. "Trust me. You'll love it. Follow me. There's a huge oak tree in the back garden with a bench under it. Perfect place to keep cool on such a hot day."

They followed a path around the side of the house, leading directly into the garden. Most of the lawn had been dug up to make room for one of the most magnificent gardens Hodgins laid eyes on. The oak tree sat at the back, with a wooden bench under the tree's canopy. Mrs. Nelson popped out the back door with two glasses of light brown liquid.

"Madam, I must compliment you on your gardening skills. This rivals anything at the Horticultural Gardens."

She blushed. "It's not that grand, but thank you. I enjoy working in it." She handed Hodgins and Billy their glasses of iced tea and went back inside.

Hodgins took a tiny sip from the glass. "It's better than expected, but I still prefer it hot. Nice on a day like this, though." He took a larger sip, then sat the glass on the bench.

Billy downed half his tea before speaking. "I'm guessing it's information yer looking for. Whatcha need now?"

"Have you heard any rumours about people smuggling gemstones in or out of the city?"

"This to do with them robberies I read about?"

"Yes. The thefts seem to tie in with a couple of murders. We've not let that information get into the newspapers, so I can't tell you anything about that." He held up a hand as Billy opened his mouth to ask questions. "I'll give you the full story when I can. What can you tell me?"

"Nothin'. I'll ask 'round. Got a few people in mind that may know something. Smuggling, eh? Probably coming in on ships. I can hang around the docks and see if I can pick up anything there. Promise you'll tell me the full story when yer done?"

"Yes, of course." Hodgins chuckled. "I made a similar promise to the lad at the paper who delivers the mail."

"Charlie? Yeah, he wants to be a reporter. I ain't got the aspirations for that."

Hodgins raised an eyebrow. "Aspirations?"

"Hey, I know some big words. You give me the information, and I'll pass it to Charlie. I don't fancy being a reporter, just like to hear the news first."

The detective drank a little more of the iced tea. "This isn't bad. Can't see it catching on, though." He looked around the garden. "It's nice to meet you somewhere other than hidden in Mitchell's stable. And this is a very nice place."

"Still gotta be careful. Plenty of the wrong sort that know me and wouldn't take kindly to seeing me talking to a rozzer."

"Yes, I understand. Suppose you'll have to be extra careful until the older thugs die off. Not a good life to be living, but at least you're out of it." Hodgins hesitated, eyebrow cocked. "Right?"

"Right. Ain't interested in anythin' 'cept information. No dodgy dealings." Billy crossed his heart. "Promise."

"Fine. If you find anything helpful, come or send someone to either the station or my home. G'day, Billy." Hodgins rose, took one last look around the garden, and went back to the station.

CHAPTER TWENTY-ONE

Once again, Hodgins rose early and boarded the train to Aurora. This time, instead of just a horse, he rented a gig with a folding cover. The sun blasted down from a sky with no clouds, and no hint of a cooling breeze. He wouldn't be able to make the trip to Lemonville quite as fast with the gig, but it would be much more comfortable and definitely easier on his still tender rump.

When he arrived at the farm where Van Dijk worked, he went to the house first, instead of the barn, as a courtesy to the landowners. He spotted Emma in the front garden with a few girlfriends. When she noticed him, she whispered something to her friends. They all giggled.

"Good morning. Emma, is it?"

She nodded.

"Do you remember me?"

"Yes. The policemen from the city."

All the girls giggled again.

"I'd like to speak with Mr. Van Dijk, if it's not an inconvenience." Hodgins stepped down from the buggy and nodded at Emma's friends.

Another round of giggles.

"Hendrik's gone. Left a note for Papa. He's in the house." Emma frowned. "Hendrik didn't even say goodbye."

"Gone? That's strange. Thank you, Emma." As he turned towards the house, one of the girls whispered not too softly to Emma, but he only caught Emma's reply.

"You're right. He's very handsome."

Hodgins grinned as the girls burst into a fit of giggles. *That will be Sara in a few more years. Heaven help me.*

The front door opened as he walked up the porch steps. "Mr. Cook? I'm Detective Hodgins. Might I have a word?"

"My wife said you were here yesterday. If you're looking for Van Dijk, you're too late. Snuck off during the night."

"So I understand. Your daughter said he left a note. Did he mention where he was headed? It's imperative I speak with him again."

"No. Just that he was sorry, but a family matter came up and he had to leave."

"Family matter? I did tell him two acquaintances from the Netherlands have been killed. He didn't mention if they were related. Could he be planning on heading back?"

"Don't know. Don't care. He's left me a man short with a newborn foal and an ailing mare. She might not make it. Now, if you don't mind, I've matters to see to." Cook closed the screen door and stepped past Hodgins.

Before the detective had a chance to leave, the door opened again. Mrs. Cook joined him on the porch with two glasses of lemonade. "Sit a moment. It's hot, and you've a long ride back. Please excuse my husband. He's worried about the mare."

"Thank you, ma'am." He took the glass, which quickly became covered in condensation. "Your daughter seems upset that Van Dijk left suddenly."

"Yes." She smiled. "I think she has a schoolgirl crush on him. A tall stranger with an accent unfamiliar to us." She blushed. "And rather dashing as well."

"I suppose that would cause a girl's head to turn at any age." *Even a married woman.* "Your husband said Van Dijk didn't say where he was going. Do you have any thoughts where he might head?"

"Well, he did mention a few times he missed home. I don't believe he spent much of his earnings, so he may have decided it was time to return now that his friends have died."

"It's possible." *Or he might be involved with the thefts or murders and is either making a run for it, or contacting the rest of the gang.*

He handed the now-empty glass back. "Thank you for the lemonade. I hope your mare pulls through."

As he placed one foot on the gig step, he tipped his homburg at the girls. "Have a pleasant day, ladies."

The giggles faded as the horse trotted down to the main road.

* * *

Barnes joined Hodgins in his office as soon as the detective returned. "Did you discover anything interesting, sir?"

"As a matter of fact, yes. Seems Van Dijk slunk off during the night. Question is, why? Guilt? Sorrow? The landowner's wife said he'd expressed a desire to return to the Netherlands. It's possible with the death of his two friends, he didn't feel like staying. Check and see what ships are scheduled to head that way. Hopefully, there wasn't one that just left."

"You think he's involved and is trying to escape?"

"The thought crossed my mind. I also wonder if he's come into the city to meet with other people involved. I just can't find a definite link between the thefts and murders. Only supposition. We do know there was to be a meeting with a third person."

"Excuse me." Sergeant Cooper stood at Hodgin's door holding a piece of paper.

Hodgins waved him in.

"Lad left a note for you. Said the girl from the boarding house sent him." Cooper handed the note to the detective and left.

"Go flag down a cabriolet and hurry. I'll explain on the way."

Hodgins gathered his notebook and stray notes, then headed out behind Barnes. A cabriolet came down the street. The constable stood on the road, waving for it to stop. Hodgins gave the driver the address on King Street and got in.

"We may have caught a break, Barnes. The char girl at the Dutchmen's lodgings sent word someone came looking for Dekker. She's going to try to keep him there. Just hope he's not impatient and leaves before we arrive."

A quarter hour later they pulled up. "Barnes, you stay here. If he's still inside, I don't want him to see the uniform yet."

Hodgins hurried up the steps and knocked on the door. Abby answered right away. As soon as she saw who it was, her shoulders slumped.

"I tried to keep him here. Said Dekker stepped out on an errand and wouldn't be long. Brought him tea and cakes. Ran next door to fetch Sammy. He's their son and is sweet on me. He took the note to the station. When I came back, the man was snooping around. Asked which room was Dekker's. Tol' him I couldn't say, as Dekker wasn't in. He stayed another few minutes then left."

"Appreciate you trying. Do you have a minute to give Constable Barnes a description?"

"Yes. Mr. Thompson is out, so he won't be yelling at me to git back to work." Abby smiled. "He's not very tolerant."

Hodgins called for Barnes to come in. While he made a sketch based on Abby's description, Hodgins had another look through both Dekker's and Jorginsen's rooms.

Even though they'd taken all their belongings to the police station, he wondered about a hiding place, berating himself for not thinking of that earlier. Jorginsen was afraid enough to sew gems into his clothing, so maybe he hid something in his room. Hodgins made his way around the space, tapping on the walls, and stomping on the floor, searching for a hiding place. He found nothing in Jorginsen's room and moved to Dekker's.

As he walked past the bed, one of the floorboards gave a little. He pulled a small knife from his trousers pocket and knelt beside the bed. Hodgins opened the blade and pried the board. It moved a little. Pressing harder, the end of the board popped up. With the hiding place revealed, the detective grasped the end and pulled the board right out.

Nestled in the gap sat a small tin box. He shook it. Something moved. Hodgins lifted the lid, hoping to find a pouch with more gemstones. Instead, the tin box contained several letters. The writing was different from the letters his sister sent. After he put the floorboard back in place, he continued tapping and stomping around the room, hoping to discover another hiding place. Satisfied there was nothing else, he joined Barnes and Abby in the front parlour.

"Almost finished." Barnes continued to sketch while Hodgins peered over his shoulder. Barnes turned the sketch so Abby could see. "Is this him?"

"Yes, yes. That's the man who came in." Abby nodded, grinning from ear to ear.

Barnes tore the page out and handed it to Hodgins.

"Very nice. As soon as we get back—"

"Take a photograph and make copies to distribute to the lads. Shall I fetch a cab?" Barnes grinned when he finished the sentence.

"Unless you want to walk back in this heat, yes." Hodgins turned to Abby. "Once again, you've been quite helpful. I hope Thompson knows what an asset you are."

"Doubt it, but thank you. This is exciting. What else can I do?"

"Just keep your eyes and ears open. G'day, Abby." He reached in his pocket and gave her a coin. She stood staring at it, mouth open.

Hodgins smiled and went out to wait while Barnes searched for a cabriolet or carriage to take them back.

CHAPTER TWENTY-TWO

Hodgins went into his office to wait for Riddell to photograph the sketch and make copies. In no time, with Jonesy's help, Riddell had twenty copies to pass around the station. He gave two to Hodgins, knowing he would give one to *The Globe*.

"That didn't take long. Has the process somehow become quicker?"

"No, sir. I took two photographs. I used one plate and gave the other to Jonesy so we could both make the copies. Twice the prints in half the time."

"Good thinking. Has he been passing along anything that will help you with the photographs?"

"He's introduced me to the gentleman who's been teaching him. Name's Fenner. Got a very nice photography shop. I'm going to save up and buy a camera for myself. He lent me a few copies of *The Philadelphia Photographer*. Didn't even know there was such a thing. Maybe the chief will approve the station getting a subscription?"

"I'll mention it. I don't think I'm in his good books at the moment, so I'll save that discussion for a later date. You know what to do with the rest of the copies. I've scribbled something for the newspaper. I'll take it down now, then head home. Hopefully, Billy will come in soon with a tip and we can make an arrest."

The constable nodded and handed out the photographic copies while Hodgins took one of the images to the newspaper.

* * *

By the time the detective arrived home, he was tired and sweaty. "Who wants to go for a swim? Seems like a perfect day to visit the beach by High Park. Maybe a picnic, too? I've hired a carriage, so you'd better say yes."

Cordelia wiped a loose lock of hair off her forehead. "That sounds wonderful. The girls have been quite cranky with this heat. The fresh air and exercise will do them good. I'll pack a basket while you gather them up."

Twenty minutes later, Hodgins and Cordelia hurried the three girls and Scraps into the waiting carriage. Sara was placed in charge of keeping Scraps out of the picnic basket. Not surprising, the beach was packed when they arrived.

Hodgins halted the horse behind a long row of buggies and carriages, then they made their way down to the sandy beach. Cordelia took the twins into one of the wooden six-foot-high, eight-foot-wide carts placed around the shore. Each summer they were rolled a few feet into the water, giving bathers a place to change into their swimming costumes. Sara found an empty bathing machine nearby, while Hodgins had to wade a bit further down, tying Scraps to a wheel on his cart.

After an hour of splashing and swimming, they changed and made their way to a grassy area to eat. All thoughts of jewel thefts and murder forgotten as the detective enjoyed a much-needed break. They lingered until the sun began to set. The twins and dog slept all the way home. Sara helped put them to bed, then retired to her room to sketch.

Hodgins and Cordelia settled in the front room, exhausted, but relaxed. "I needed that. What with the trips north and running around the city, my mind was reeling. And I'm certain you needed a break as well."

Cordelia fanned her face with a copy of *Ladies' Home Magazine*. "We should do that more often. I almost fell asleep more than once from the heat. Not even a breeze coming through the windows. Now tell me, what did your trip to Lemonville this morning reveal?"

"The man I went to see has done a runner. Still trying to discover if it was because he's part of the thefts and murders, or because his friends have died and he misses his homeland." He smacked his forehead. "How could I have forgotten? I went back to the boarding house where the Dutchmen stayed and found some letters hidden under the floorboards. They're still in my suit jacket." Hodgins had draped his jacket over the arm of the chair, so he didn't need to drag his weary body to the row of hooks by the front door. He reached into the pocket and pulled the stack of letters out.

Cordelia stopped fanning. "Who are they from?"

"Only one way to find out." He lifted the flap and removed the first one, glancing at the end of the letter first.

Fortunately, they were written in English. "Someone called Bonney."

"Bonnie? A woman?" Cordelia forgot about the heat and stood behind her husband's chair so she could read along.

"Likely a last name, like William Bonney." Hodgins snickered.

"What's so funny? Saying the name made it sound like a woman."

"William Bonney. Billy the Kid. I know you've heard of him."

"Oh." Her eyes widened. "Oh! Do you think he's involved? Shouldn't you let people know he's in Toronto?" She rushed to the doorway. "Are the children safe?"

"Calm yourself, Delia. Billy the Kid is a train and bank robber. As far as I know, he doesn't go around killing people and stuffing them in whisky barrels. Must be hundreds of people with the name Bonney. If you're worried, go upstairs and sit with them while I read the letters."

Once Cordelia left, Hodgins removed his notebook and pencil from the jacket and wrote *Bonney* on a fresh page. He spent the next two hours reading and re-reading, jotting notes, and thinking.

He slumped in the chair, waking with a start when the notebook slid off his lap. The mantle clock chimed twice. Rubbing his eyes, he squinted at the time. "Good Lord!" He stood, placed the letters, notebook, and pencil on the seat of the chair, and headed to bed.

* * *

Oversleeping the next morning, he quickly dressed and ran down the stairs, almost tripping over Scraps, napping at the foot of the staircase. He cut a thick slice of bread, smeared some homemade apple jelly on it, then ran out the door as he stuffed the letters and notebook into his pocket. Racing across Lowther Avenue, Hodgins was lucky enough to spot an empty cabriolet coming down Avenue Road, headed towards Bloor Street. He flagged it down, arriving at the Station House a quarter of an hour later.

"Barnes, fetch me a cup of tea, would you? Then join me in my office."

By the time Barnes returned, Hodgins had the letters spread out across his desk. "We've got another name. Unfortunately, I've no clue who he is." He handed one of the letters to the constable. "They're signed Bonney." He waited for a response, knowing Henry enjoyed reading stories about the robbers in the United States. It only took a second.

"Billy the Kid? Can't be. Last I read, he was in Texas. Around the Guadalupe Mountains."

"Yes, I rather doubt it's him. Have you come across that name? Have any of you? Get Harrington and Riddell in here. We need to put our heads together."

As the constables grabbed their notes and gathered in Hodgins' office, young Billy arrived. The small office became quite crowded.

Hodgins let the young lad start. "What have you, Billy? Good news, I hope."

"Found out there's a new gang trying to take over the docks. Goes by the name South Shore Goons. Led by an American called Bonebreaker Bonney. No one seems to know much about him."

"Bonney? Just came across that name last night. Finally, something that connects. Now, we just need to figure out who this Bonebreaker is. Anything else?"

"No, but I'll keep looking." He turned to the constables and with a flourish, removed his tweed newsboy cap. "Gentlemen." Billy smiled, then headed out, whistling *Camptown Races.*

"Strange boy." Harrington shook his head. "Ain't that the street boy, Backstreet Billy? How'd he get the money to buy a nice tweed hat?"

"Got himself a job at the newspaper. He's a smart lad. Enough about Billy." Hodgins waved his arm across his desk. "Found a stack of letters hidden in Dekker's room. All signed by someone called Bonney. We need to find him. Maybe he's the person who came to the boarding house. We have a description and a name, just don't know if they're the same person. Riddell, you check with Sergeant Cooper. See who's working the dock area in the evening and let them know about the South Shore Goons."

Riddell reached for his walking stick.

"Not now. We need to come up with some sort of plan first. If this Bonney chap is American and involved with the smuggling, he likely came up from either New York or Boston. Since I've got a passing acquaintance with the police in both cities. I'll prepare telegrams, then have a quick chat with Abby at the boarding house. See if she thinks the man who came in was American. People from New York and Boston have very distinct speech patterns. Unmistakable. Barnes, take the photo you have and ask around the docks. Let whichever constable is making day rounds down there know. Is one of the dates on the list of ship arrivals today?"

Barnes nodded. "I'll check. There is one this week, just don't recall which day."

"Good. Harrington, you have a copy of the photo of the man looking for Dekker?"

"Yes."

"Good. You ask around the train station. Since the person looking for Dekker didn't meet him, he might be planning on leaving town. After I speak with the char girl at the boarding house, I'll have a word with the dockmaster. Let him know there may be a gang trying to stir up trouble."

"Sir? What should I do after getting the name of the constable on night duty around the docks?" Riddell leaned forward, both hands on the carved lion on top of his walking stick.

"See if you can track him down. He's likely still in bed, so wait a bit. Meanwhile, take a look at the list of United Loyalist members and see if any of them have ties to the States. There has to be a reason Dekker's body was left at that club."

None of the constables moved. The detective stood. "Well, are you waiting for? An invitation? Off with you."

Barnes and Harrington took off. Riddell waited as he didn't move as fast with the bad leg, then went to speak with Sergeant Cooper. Hodgins listened to the rhythm of one footstep, followed by the thump of the stick. *Lad's lucky he can still walk. At least he's no longer depressed.*

Hodgins walked to Parliament Street and flagged down a cab to take him to the boarding house. All types of buggies, carriages, and gigs filled the street, making the trip a little longer than expected. After diverting around two buggies with locked wheels, they finally arrived. As he stepped off, he turned to the driver, well known to him. "Please wait, Bert. I'll only be a few minutes."

"Right oh, detective." Bert dropped the reins in his lap and closed his eyes.

Abby waved from the porch as Hodgins came up the walk. "Hello, detective. Did you find the fella yet?"

"Good morning, Abby. No, but I have a question about him. Did you notice anything different about his speech? The way he talked. An accent?"

Her eyes lit up. "Yeah. He didn't say much, but he didn't say his r's."

"Didn't say them at all, or pronounced them like ah?"

Abby thought a minute, eyes narrowed as she tried to remember. "No, not ah. I met someone from Boston once. She talked like that. This fella didn't sound like that at all."

"Thank you, Abby. That's all I wondered. G'day."

Hodgins left her to continue sweeping the porch, patting the horse before entering the cab. "Take me to the harbourmaster, Bert."

The streets were busier, now that the businesses were open. The wealthy non-working gentry would still be at home, but businessmen and servants rushed around the stores. The trip took a little longer than usual, but Hodgins was in no rush.

"Want me ta wait?" Bert halted the chestnut mare so the detective could get off.

"No. Don't know how long I'll be." He tossed a few coins to Bert, patted the horse again, then went in search of the harbourmaster. A few ships had come in, so it took over a half hour to locate him.

"Sorry, Detective, but I'm quite busy. Got ships trying to load around others unloading, and half of them don't speak English."

"This will only take a minute. I just want to let you know about some information that's come my way. There's a rumour a gang has been around the docks. Possibly smugglers, maybe worse."

"Ain't no rumour. Been more fights than usual these past few weeks. Saw two men take off carrying a crate before I could check it. Buggers got away. I've got extra men keeping watch. If there's real trouble, you'll hear about it."

"I'll be telling my constables to keep an eye on the docks when they're patrolling, especially at night. There was a scuffle a week ago, and shortly after, a body was found by Gooderham's. It's possible the two are connected."

"The man in the whisky barrel? I read about that."

"Yes. A constable heard the commotion, but they left before he could find them. Timeframe fits. Please let the police know right away if there's trouble."

Raised voices caused both men to turn. Three men argued and gestured. Only one spoke English.

"That's one of my men." The harbourmaster turned to leave.

"Wait, just one more thing." Hodgins pulled the photograph from his jacket pocket. "Have you seen this man hanging around?"

"No. Thanks for the warning about the gang, but we're coping just fine." He hurried towards the three men, leaving the detective standing on the dock.

Hodgins walked back to the small office the harbourmaster kept and left the photograph on the messy desk, along with a short note, then walked back to the station. He needed time alone to think. Try to tie the murders and thefts together. When he arrived at King Street, he detoured to the second jewellery store robbed to find out if the additional security the owner hired had news.

Mr. Morrison showed a pair of earrings to a customer, so Hodgins had to wait. The customer left without making a purchase, putting Morrison in a bad mood.

"Detective, are you here to tell me you finally found my gems?"

"No. We're still following up. I was in the area and wanted to know if the man you hired to watch the stores overnight has anything to report?"

"Other than drunks? No. His presence might have scared the thief off this section of King, though. Heard tell Fitzsimmons got hit."

"Unfortunately. Your man didn't notice anything at all?"

"Never mentioned seeing anyone."

"Anything he saw or heard could be important. Could you tell me how I can contact him?"

Morrison sighed. "Wasting your time." He tore a page off a small pad and wrote a name and address. "He's only just gone home a couple of hours ago."

"Thank you, Mr. Morrison. Have you put a lock on the upstairs door yet?"

"Yesterday. Not locking my office during the day, though."

"That's entirely up to you. It was only a suggestion. I'll be in touch when we recover your items."

Hodgins placed the paper in his notebook, making a mental note to visit the security man later, if necessary, then continued to the station.

Riddell sat at his desk going through the membership list for the Loyalist Club.

"Barnes and Harrington not back yet?"

"No, sir. But I did find one interesting thing going through this list. Seems three of the members have family in the States. Oh, I found the constable doing night rounds at the docks. He hasn't seen anything out of the ordinary."

Hodgins nodded. "Any of the family in New York? From the description of the way the man looking for

Dekker spoke, and char girl's comment on his speech, I think he may be American. Possibly from New York."

"Two in New York. The other has family in Michigan."

"Hopefully, one of them will provide a connection, or maybe even a motive. When Barnes and Harrington return, bring them to my office."

Five minutes later, Cooper knocked on Hodgins' door. "Telegram. From New York."

"Good news, I hope." He took the envelope and opened it. His smile widened as he read. "Very good news indeed."

CHAPTER TWENTY-THREE

The detective updated his notes with the details from the telegram. The message was short, but gave him the information he needed. *Will I have to make another trip into the United States? What's taking Barnes and Harrington so long?*

His last question was answered when the door opened, letting in a blast of heat and two weary, bedraggled constables. Hodgins watched as Riddell grabbed his walking stick and met his fellow constables midway across the room. The three of them made their way to his office, Riddell moving faster than the others for a change.

Hodgins took in the appearance of Barnes and Harrington. "What the devil happened to you two?"

"Have you been outside, sir? It's a lot hotter than this morning." Barnes removed his police helmet and dragged a hanky across his forehead before replacing it.

"Leave the helmets off for now and unbutton the top of your uniform. Cool off if at all possible before going to your desks. I spoke to the harbourmaster, and he already knew about the gang. Didn't see you when I was down there, Barnes. Did you have a chance to speak with the dock workers?"

Barnes took his notebook out and flipped to the last few written pages. "Yes. Some saw what they called 'suspicious actions,' but couldn't, or wouldn't, say anything specific. Most had heard rumours about a gang. Some recognized the man in the picture as a recruiter who spoke to them. A couple of the larger workers admitted they were approached to join, but declined. I imagine more were also asked to join, but didn't give up that information. Was surprised that the ones who mentioned it told me. If it got around they said anything, they'd likely get a good beating."

"Don't suppose you got a name?" The detective tapped his pencil on the desktop.

Barnes shook his head.

"That's something, at least. Harrington? Any luck at the train station?"

"Afraid not, sir. If this other fella came in weeks ago, no one remembers. He's just an average-looking bloke, and we've not got a description of Van Dijk, so we don't know if he's taken a train."

Hodgins dropped the pencil and leaned back. "How stupid of me. Of course we need a description of him. Should've taken Barnes to Lemonville." He turned to his senior constable. "When we're done here, stay back and I'll give you a description of Van Dijk. He may have booked passage on a ship home, or taken the train across the border. More ships in New York and Boston."

"The telegram, sir?" Riddell pointed at the envelope on the detective's desk.

"I believe we may have caught a break." He slid it to the edge of his desk and nodded at Riddell to pick it up. "It's from the detective with the New York Police. There's a criminal family named Bonney in Brooklyn. One daughter married a Canadian. He's trying to find a name. Maybe it will match up with a member of the Loyalist Club, or possibly an employee at Gooderham and Worts. Riddell, the three names you found on the member list with American ties, any married?"

Riddell went through his notes. "Yes, two. The one in Michigan, and one of the New Yorkers. You want me to visit and find out the maiden names of the wives?"

Hodgins touched the tip of his nose. "Spot on." He reached into his pocket and drew out several coins. "Here. Get a cab. Have him wait at both homes. Save you finding another, and will give the horse a break to rest under a tree. It's getting late, so take the cabriolet home when you're done. Don't want your mother seeing you looking like these two. She'll have my hide. Nothing left now except wait. Harrington, helmet and buttons before you leave my office. Barnes, you got what you need to make a sketch?"

"Could use a larger pad, but I can use my book again."

"Here." Hodgins reached into his desk and pulled out the pad of foolscap. "Use this."

Barnes accepted the larger pad and settled back in his chair, ready to sketch. "Remind me why this size is called foolscap. An odd name for paper."

"It's quite simple, really. Back in the 15th century in Germany, the larger-sized paper had the watermark of a fool's cap on it. Like the old court jesters wore. Surely, you've seen drawings of it."

"Those funny hats with bells on the tips? Yes. Strange thing to use for a watermark. I'm ready now. You can start anytime."

Hodgins closed his eyes to visualize Van Dijk before speaking. After an hour of sketching and erasing, Barnes had a finished drawing.

"I can see some similarities between this chap and Dekker and Jorginsen. The long, broad face, and they're all tall, which won't show up in the sketch. You said he's also blond and blue-eyed. I can use coloured pencils for the sketch, like I did with Dekker. Unfortunately, the photograph won't show that. The only real difference is the mole in front of Van Dijk's left ear. Strange, it's almost in the same place as Dekker's scar. Only about an inch off. Shall I go out and ask the char girl if he's visited?"

"It's almost the end of your shift. Wait until tomorrow. She'll likely be busy cleaning the house before she's allowed to go home, and no doubt the landlord will be there. He won't take kindly to you keeping her from her chores."

"I can go first thing and wait for her to arrive, or the landlord to leave."

"Best wait for him to leave. Abby likely won't arrive until just before she's expected. If he keeps to the routine I've seen, he'll have a leisurely breakfast before going out. Wait until, say, ten. Maybe by then the New York Police will have discovered who this Bonney girl married, and Riddell will provide the final connection."

* * *

When Hodgins arrived at the station in the morning, he checked with Sergeant Cooper to see if a telegram came in. "Blast. I'd hoped there'd be word. Even if Riddell found something, a reply from New York connecting the name to the family there would make the case stronger."

"I'll let you know as soon as it comes in."

Hodgins stood at the sergeant's desk, thinking. "You know, we haven't found any of the jewels stolen in Toronto. The ones sewn into Jorginsen's suit couldn't be from here, unless someone didn't report the theft. Dekker is likely the thief from Cobb's, but we didn't find the items on his body or in his room at the boarding house. And the last two robberies were done after his death. Just how many people are we looking for?"

Cooper shrugged. "Wish I could help."

Hodgins knocked on the top of the desk. "So do I. Someone must know something." He went into his office to wait for Riddell to arrive.

Barnes was the first of his constables to come in. "Riddell not here yet?"

"No. Expect him anytime. I hope he's got some good news." Hodgins turned when he heard laughing. Riddell and Harrington came in together.

"Detective! I've found something." Riddell joined Hodgins and Barnes, Harrington on his heels.

155

"Been after him for two blocks to tell me, but he wouldn't say a word." Harrington nudged Riddell's shoulder, then turned to Hodgins. "Your office for an update?"

"No. It's quiet enough here until the rest of the lads come in. What have you found, Tom?"

"Well, it's not an exact connection, but Mr. Hale's wife is from Brooklyn, and her best friend growing up had an older sister named Francine Bonney. Francine moved to Canada after her marriage, too. Mrs. Hale couldn't, or wouldn't, confirm it's the same Bonney family the New York Police say are criminals. She did say she thought the husband was involved with a distillery."

Both Barnes and Harrington cheered.

"Not so fast. I need to send another telegram to Captain Harrison with Miss Bonney's name." *Hope he isn't holding a grudge from when I tossed him out of the city. Or is that why his replies are slow and with little information?* "If he doesn't reply today, I'll have to go down, and that will cost a few days we don't have. The next ship on that list is due in and back out soon. If it leaves with the missing jewels, we'll never find them or the killer."

"Sir, remember that newspaper I found in the alley by Gooderham and Worts? It was from Brooklyn." Barnes flipped through his notes. "The *Brooklyn Daily Eagle.*"

"And I've seen that newspaper since. A full edition. I'll send a telegram to Harrison with two names for him to check. I believe we're closing in."

CHAPTER TWENTY-FOUR

Another day passed before Hodgins received an answer to his telegram. The link he hoped for finally arrived. He put together all the information he had, along with the telegram, and put in a request for a search warrant. By the afternoon, he had it.

"Barnes, Harrington, with me. We have a house to search and an arrest to make."

Harrington ran ahead to Parliament Street to hail a passing carriage to take them to Lennox Street. A stern-looking woman in her forties answered the door.

Detective Hodgins handed her the warrant. "We need to search your home. Please stand aside."

She glanced at the paper. "My husband isn't here. You can't just barge in and search through my home."

"That paper says otherwise." Hodgins stepped around her, followed by Barnes and Harrington. "Be thorough, and check for hidden places in the walls and floors. Harrington, check the rooms at the front, and make sure she doesn't go anywhere. Barnes, go through everything in the kitchen. I'll check the bedrooms."

Two hours later, Hodgins had the constables take the woman to the station, while he flagged down a passing cabriolet and headed to Gooderham and Worts.

He entered the office and went straight to the assistant's desk. "David Bowdre, I'm placing you under arrest on suspicion of murder and theft."

Gooderham overhead and rushed out of his office. "What's the meaning of this? You can't just burst in here and arrest my clerk."

"I'm afraid I can. I have proof he's involved with several jewellery store robberies, and is suspected of the murder of two men." Hodgins placed Bowdre in handcuffs and walked him to the waiting cabriolet.

Mr. Gooderham stood in the doorway watching as his long-time employee was whisked away.

Bowdre complained all the way to the station. "I'm not a thief, and most certainly have not murdered anyone. I'll have your badge for this."

Hodgins ignored the ranting, calling out for the driver to push the horse as fast as possible all the way up Parliament Street. Few people were on the street to hear the commotion as most of the way were houses, occupants at work.

Once at the station, Bowdre refused to move. It took two constables to wrangle him out. Hodgins casually strolled behind the tussle, smiling all the way to the interrogation room.

"Mr. Bowdre, if you're not involved in the thefts, can you explain why this was found at your residence?" The detective opened a small cloth bag that one of the constables had placed on the table. He poured out dozens of loose gemstones.

"Those are mine. Bought them weeks ago. Was going to have them made into a necklace for my wife."

"Interesting. The size, quantity, and I suspect the quality just happen to exactly match what was stolen from Cobb's jewellery store. Can you produce a receipt for your purchase?"

Bowdre stammered. "Receipt? I… no, but…"

"Surely you planned on insuring the necklace once finished? An insurance company would require proof of ownership. A receipt from the person setting the stones wouldn't be enough. Tell me, where were you on the tenth of this month?"

"At home, with my wife. She'll confirm that."

"And you never left all evening? Didn't go to the United Loyalist Club?"

"I told you. I was home all evening. Never went out until morning when I went to work. Besides, I'm not a member of that club."

"That's true. I have a copy of the membership list, and you're not on it. You are, however, friends with Mr. Hale, who *is* a member. His wife's childhood friend is from Brooklyn, as are you. This friend is the daughter of a known criminal, who's elder sister just happens to be your wife. I recall seeing the *Brooklyn Daily Eagle* at the distillery and you telling me your parents are still there. I suppose you'll deny knowing the Bonney family?"

"Yes. I mean, no. I don't deny knowing *of* the family. Doesn't mean we were friends."

Hodgins scooped up the gems and placed them back in the cloth bag. "I believe I'll have a chat with your wife." He rose and opened the door. "Constable, take Mr. Bowdre to the cells and bring his wife up."

"My wife?" Bowdre stood, knocking the chair back. "You rotter. Throwing my wife in your filthy cells? You'll pay for that."

"Constable, you'd better cuff him before leading him down."

Hodgins sat, taking a ruby from the sack. *Very nice. These would make a spectacular piece of jewellery.*

A few minutes passed before Mrs. Bowdre was brought in, uncuffed. She made no fuss, and the insults she'd shouted when at home had finally stopped.

"Mrs. Bowdre. Can you tell me where you and your husband were on the tenth of this month? Thursday of last week?"

She crossed her arms and remained silent.

"I see. You do realize we know these gems are stolen?" The detective picked up the bag and gave it a shake. "Since they were found in your home, you're just as guilty as your husband. You'll spend years in jail. I also know your maiden name is Bonney. The same Bonney family from Brooklyn, who are well-known to the police down there. Two men we strongly believe are connected to the thefts and smuggling have been murdered."

Hodgins watched her, hoping for a tell-tale response. Nothing, so he continued.

"Your brother has formed a gang and is currently here in Toronto. We can place him at the docks. If your husband is connected to the murders, as well as the robberies, he'll hang. It's possible a jury will find you guilty as well. Being an accomplice carries almost as much risk as committing the crime. You may not hang, but you'll be in jail for a very long time."

He studied her face and posture as he spoke. She'd uncrossed her arms, and her shoulders relaxed. The smug look left her face.

Is she finally admitting defeat? "If you're willing to tell us what you know, I can't promise you won't see the inside of the prison, but your sentence will be lighter. It's your decision. Say nothing and face the consequences, or tell me everything, and it will reduce your time behind bars. Last Thursday?"

"You can promise my sentence will be light?"

"Yes, ma'am. The judge will take that into consideration." *Please tell me my suspicions are right.*

"Last Thursday, Benny came to the house."

"Benny?"

"My brother, Benjamin. When I married and moved to Canada, I thought I'd left the stigma of my family behind. Two weeks ago, Benny showed up with one of his schemes. He and my husband were childhood friends, but David wanted something other than a criminal life. Didn't want to be on the run, in hiding all the time. We moved here, and he got a good job at the distillery. He's respected, and we have a nice home, but he's been trying to save money to return to Brooklyn to take care of his parents."

"When your brother came, did they stay home?"

She shook her head. "No, they went out and hadn't returned by the time I retired for the night. I swear I knew nothing about the robberies or murder."

"And the previous Sunday? Can you recall that evening?"

"Yes. That's the first time Benny showed up at my home. I didn't know he'd come to Canada. He arrived quite late. They went into the study and closed the door. About a half hour later they went out. David said nothing to me before leaving. After he left for work in the morning, I tidied up and discovered his jacket pocket was ripped. I sewed it up, curious how it happened, but afraid to ask."

Hodgins wrote down everything she said, thoughts running through his mind. *Was it Bonney and Bowdre Constable Duggan heard on the docks? Did both men murder Jorginsen?*

"When your husband returned home Thursday, did you find anything odd about his clothing? More rips? Any blood?"

"No." Her voice trembled, barely a whisper.

I don't believe she's involved. Not even after the fact. "Thank you, Mrs. Bowdre. Is there anything else you can think of?"

"That's everything. I haven't seen my brother since."

Hodgins made a few more notes, then closed his book. "I don't believe you're involved in all this. I'll have a constable take you home and watch your house in case your brother tries to contact you again. Please do not attempt to leave town."

He escorted her to the front and told Harrington to take her home and keep watch for Bonney, then had her husband brought back to the interrogation room.

"Mr. Bowdre, tell me about your meetings with Benjamin Bonney."

"Don't know who you're referring to." He crossed his arms and looked at the wall.

"Your brother-in-law. Your wife was quite forthcoming when faced with the prospect of jail. You met with him a week ago Sunday, and again last Thursday. Went out with him and returned late. Coincides with both murders. If you confess, you may not hang, but you will be in jail for a long, long time. Your wife would be able to quietly return to Brooklyn if she wishes, rather than jail as an accomplice."

Bowdre said nothing, but one eyebrow shot up. He uncrossed his arms and gripped the edge of the table.

He hadn't considered what would happen to his wife. Now, he's thinking. "I can tie you to the robbery at Cobb's with these gems. If you're involved with the smuggling, tell me where the rest of the jewels are. There were two other break-ins, and those gems were not found in your house."

His suspect sighed, finally admitting to partial participation. "I wasn't involved in the thefts. Bonney asked me to hide the gems you found. I don't know where the rest are."

"And you've nothing more to add."

Bowdre leaned back. "Nothing."

Hodgins stood and went to the door. "Constable, escort Mr. Bowdre back to the cell." He turned to Bowdre. "Think about your options. Think about your wife. I *will* tie you to the murders. If you don't confess, you'll hang for sure."

CHAPTER TWENTY-FIVE

odgins returned the gems to the small safe in the evidence room and went into his office to review his notes. He closed the door to avoid interruptions, noticing Barnes look up when the door clicked shut. The detective shook his head, indicating he didn't want to be disturbed.

I'm missing something. But what? He placed the sheet of foolscap he'd made notes on beside his notebook. Everything the constables found had been added to his book. One of them must have the missing piece to tie Bowdre to the murders. *Hale.* An indirect connection, but maybe he or his wife saw or heard something of use. *I need to speak with Mrs. Hale.*

The detective went to Barnes for the list of Loyalist members to get Hale's address. He hurried to Mitchell's Livery and hired a gig rather than waiting for the trolley or searching for a passing cabriolet. The Hales lived in the north section of the city called Yorkville. When he arrived, Mrs. Hale was preparing to leave.

"It's imperative I speak with you now. Please. I can take you to your appointment when I'm done."

She hesitated, checking the time on her lapel watch. "I can delay only a short time. My friend is waiting for me at Robert Simpson's store. Come in."

"My constable spoke with you earlier. You said you had a friend in Brooklyn from the Bonney family. I need to find out more. I know of their reputation and dealings with the police. It's your friend's sister I'm here about. The sister is married to David Bowdre. Are you acquainted with her?"

"I don't care to discuss the Bonney family, detective. And Bernadette's sister is older. I knew of her, nothing more. We've had no contact in Toronto."

"And your husband has no dealings with Mr. Bowdre that you are aware of?"

"He does not discuss his business with me, as I assume you do not discuss yours with your wife."

Hodgins smiled. "Actually, my wife takes quite an interest in my work, as does my eldest daughter."

She raised an eyebrow. "I find that hard to believe."

"I can assure you it's true. My wife is well-read and has an amazing mind. I encourage her and my daughter to expand their minds and knowledge."

She leaned forward, examining his face. "I think I believe you." She paused.

The detective laughed. "My wife is strong willed. I wouldn't think of telling her what to do. She's even joined the Women's Literary Club."

Mrs. Hale raised an eyebrow at the mention of the club, but said nothing. She checked the lapel watch again, pinned to her bodice.

"I will take you to meet your friend, as promised. Where might I find your husband? I need to get more information from him."

"He works at Royal Fire and Life on Wellington Street. They don't close until 6:00 p.m. so you should find him there."

Hodgins wrote the address down then helped Mrs. Hale into the gig and took her to the store at the corner of Yonge and Queen Streets. After escorting her to the doorway, he steered the Cleveland Bay towards Hale's place of business.

Hodgins had never paid much attention to the building at the corner of Yonge and Wellington. The three-and-a-half-story structure proudly filled the space along both streets. He looked up and noticed they even had the name and date at the top. The words Royal Insurance ran along both sides, with 1861 below.

He opened the heavy oak exterior door and walked to the front desk. "Excuse me. I'm looking for Mr. Hale."

"Do you have an appointment?" The clerk opened an appointment book. "I don't see anyone listed at this time."

"No, I don't have an appointment, and now that you've told me he's free, I'd like a word." Hodgins pointed at the badge pinned to his suit jacket, then presented a calling card.

The clerk read the card. "You'll find him on the second floor. Room 202."

"Thank you." Hodgins made his way up and found his office. The door stood ajar, so he walked into the small outer office without knocking and showed his badge. "I need a word with Mr. Hale."

"One moment please, detective." The clerk opened the inner office door just enough to slip through. A minute later, the door opened wide, and the clerk stepped out. "Mr. Hale will see you now."

Hodgins walked into Hale's office, closing the door tight. He was momentarily taken aback when he saw the man. His wife was in her early thirties, and quite pleasant looking, despite her stern expression. Hale had to be at least fifteen years older, had the jowls of a hog, and the figure to match.

Hodgins extended his hand. "Sorry to interrupt your day, but I'm hoping you can assist in my inquires."

Hale stared at the hand, not making any attempt to shake it. "What inquires are those, sir?"

Hodgins sat without being invited. *Thoroughly unpleasant man.* "Some jewel thefts, murders, and an old acquaintance—Benjamin Bonney. Surely, you've read about the murders and thefts?"

Hale shook his head, jowls flapping. "I told your constable neither my wife nor myself has any connection to the Bonney family. My wife knew the family years ago. She no longer keeps in touch. If that's all?"

"No, that's not all. Are you acquainted with David Bowdre? He's the office clerk at Gooderham and Worts. His wife is a member of the Bonney family. The older sister of your wife's friend."

Hale's face paled. "My wife has told me about the Bonneys. Thoroughly despicable lot. Are you suggesting I'm somehow involved in all this? You drag my name through the streets and I'll see you lose your badge."

The detective smiled. "Not the first time I've heard that threat. I'm not trying to sully your name, just want to find the proper connections. Is it possible Benjamin Bonney paid you a visit? Attempted to involve you in his scheme? If so, as long as you turned him down, you've done nothing wrong. Two men are dead, and their families deserve justice. Please, did he approach either you or your wife?"

Hale drummed his fingertips on the desk. "Yes." The word came out with a hiss.

"What did he want? Was he specific?"

"He wanted me to let him use the club. There are rooms most don't know about. I told him it would be impossible. During the day, there's someone at the door checking membership before letting anyone in. After hours, it's locked, and I don't have a key."

"How did he know to come to you?"

"His youngest sister was a childhood friend of my wife, as you already know. They kept in touch only briefly after we moved to Canada. She gave him our address."

Hodgins scribbled some notes in his book before continuing. "And how did he react when you turned him down? Did he threaten you?"

"Yes. Said if I told anyone about his visit, it would be my wife who would pay." He shuttered. "Don't want to think what he meant by that."

"One more thing. Did Mrs. Bowdre ever visit your wife?"

"Not that she mentioned. Neither of us has ever met the Bowdres." His eyes widened. "Do you believe Bonney's sisters are involved?"

"No, I didn't get that impression, at least not from the elder one, Francine, but her brother may have threatened her to see if she could get Mrs. Hale to change your mind." The detective stood. "I don't have any further questions at the moment. If you remember anything else, please come to Station House Four. Thank you for your time."

Hodgins nodded at the clerk on his way out. He hurried down the stuffy stairwell and out the building. Hopping into the gig, he guided the Cleveland Bay around the block and over to Duke Street. When he arrived at Mitchell's Livery, instead of walking to the station, he lingered.

"Got some thinking to do. I'll take care of the horse." Hodgins unhitched the Bay and walked him to a stall. While the horse munched on hay, Hodgins wiped him down, then slowly brushed his coat.

This is more complicated than I expected. Two loose connections to an American criminal and a smuggling ring. Precious gems stolen, the likely thieves murdered. Why? Neither was caught, so why not continue to use them? Did this Bonney chap do the killing? Did he have help? Two different knives were used.

The questions swirled through his mind over and over. By the time the horse was cooled and brushed, he still had no answers.

As he made his way north to the police station, someone yelled. Hodgins looked up just in time to jump back and avoid a collision with a passing carriage, horses running hard.

"Watch where yer walking!" The driver's words were almost lost in the wind as the carriage flew past.

"Slow down before you kill someone." Hodgins recognized the carriage and driver and made a mental note to speak to the owner. Instead of the coachman, the youngest son was at the reins. "Bloody fool."

When he arrived at the police station, rather than going into his office, the detective headed for the storage room and pulled out the large, wheeled blackboard. One wheel squeaked as he pulled it into his office. Once it was positioned against a wall, he carefully printed names and drew lines. A solid line for a direct link, dashed for indirect. Most of his lines were dashes.

"Barnes."

The constable was already on his way to the detective's office. "Thought you might be calling me when the big board came out. That's quite a list of people. Are they all suspects?"

"No. I don't believe the women are involved, but they are connected to Bonney." Hodgins underlined Francine Bowdre. "This is his sister. And this…" He underlined Mrs. Hale. "This is an old friend of Francine's younger sister." He circled David Bowdre's name. "The gems stolen from Cobb were found in his house."

"What about Mr. Hale? How's he fit inta all this?

"Just had a chat with him. Bonney wanted Hale to let him hide at the United Loyalist Club. Bonney threatened his wife if he mentioned it to anyone."

"Hmm." Barnes scratched his head, messing his hair. "Do you think Dekker's body was left behind the club as a warning of sorts?"

Hodgins tapped the constable on his arm. "Yes, that's a good point. My mind's been so muddled I didn't think of that."

"But where are the rest of the stolen gems? Especially that huge diamond? We found nothing at the boarding house. And the other Dutchman. Is he involved?"

The detective picked up the chalk and drew lines between Dekker, Jorginsen, and Van Dijk. "We know they all knew each other, and that Dekker and Van Dijk were friends in the Netherlands. Don't know if Jorginsen was an old friend, family, or if they met smuggling. Has there been any sightings of Van Dijk?"

"Nothing yet. There's a ship leaving tonight that has a stop in Amsterdam. Duggan is going to make sure he goes to the dock earlier than normal on his rounds to check it out."

"I have a feeling he's simply going home and back to an old sweetheart with news of her brother. Forgot to tell Van Dijk to ask if the bodies should be shipped home. We need to figure out where Bonney is hiding. I think another visit to his sister, Mrs. Bowdre, is required."

Both the detective and constable made their way to St. Mary Street, east of Queens Park. When they arrived, the front door sat ajar. Hodgins and Barnes exchanged a look. "Go around the back, Henry. Be careful."

The detective slowly opened the door wide enough to enter. He stepped in, stopping to listen. Silence. Hodgins walked to the foot of the staircase. Again, silence. The back door opened.

"Barnes, find anything?"

"No, sir. Yard is clear. Looks like someone's been in the kitchen recently. Kettle's warm, and there's a half-drunk cup of tea on the table."

Hodgins joined him, and they both checked the second floor. "Don't hear or see anyone. Doesn't look as though the house was searched, and there's no sign of a struggle. Where could Mrs. Bowdre have gone in such a hurry she didn't close the door?"

"I'll ask the neighbours if they saw anything." Barnes went through the house and out the front door. He returned five minutes later.

Hodgins jumped when the door opened. "That was fast. Find something?"

"Sir, the lady next door said a man came, and Mrs. Bowdre left with him. Didn't appear to be forced, but he had a hold of her arm, almost dragging her. She didn't struggle or scream. The description matched Bonney. Happened about ten minutes ago. Went in the direction we came from."

CHAPTER TWENTY-SIX

Hodgins removed his homburg and smacked the side of his leg with it. "Blast! We must have passed them. I was certain she wasn't involved. Maybe he took Mrs. Bowdre to keep her husband quiet. The question is, do we tell him and hope it shakes him up enough to confess to being involved, or say nothing and tell him she's told us everything? Come on. Maybe they're going to the train station and back to New York."

They ran until they found an empty cabriolet and had the driver race to Union Station. "I wonder if there're any trains going to New York this afternoon?" Barnes bounced as the wheel hit a hole in the road.

The horse made a sharp turn onto Yonge Street. The detective grabbed the side of the cabriolet to prevent sliding into Barnes. "Not certain. I do know they route through Montreal. Nothing direct. With luck, there's not one until tonight, and they'll be waiting for it."

When they arrived, Hodgins paid the cabbie while Barnes ran in to check the schedule. "Sir, next train to Montreal is at 7:15 tonight."

The detective went to the ticket booth. "Afternoon Charlie. Looking for a man and woman who may have purchased a ticket, possibly to New York." Hodgins described them.

"Yep. They were here, oh, not twenty minutes ago. Montreal to New York. Believe I heard her suggest they have supper at the Queen's Hotel while they wait."

"She didn't seem at all nervous or upset?"

Charlie shrugged. "No more than any siblings. Heard her call him brother. Strange thing, they had no luggage with them. The brother was carrying a satchel, but it weren't big enough for clothes."

"Thanks, Charlie. You've been a big help. Come on, Henry. We've a thief to catch."

The hotel stood just down the street from the train station, so they ran as fast as they could in the heat. They entered the luxurious four-story hotel and made their way to the dining room. The detective spoke to the maître d', describing Bonney. After promising not to raise a ruckus, along with a not-so-subtle hint at an arrest for interfering in police business, he got the confirmation he needed.

"Thank you. We'll be as discreet as possible." Hodgins went back to Barnes. "They're here. Requested a table at the back, well away from the windows and front door. Probably trying to stay hidden. I doubt Bonney even knowns the police are on to him. We need to do this as quickly and quietly as possible. Don't imagine Mrs. Bowdre will be a problem, especially if she didn't go willingly."

The detective went around one side of the dining room, approaching from Bonney's back. Barnes came around the other side, both hugging the walls as much as possible. Mrs. Bowdre spotted Hodgins but didn't alert her brother. Instead, she kept him distracted, discussing the menu. Hodgins came up behind the man's chair and placed a hand on Bonney's shoulder. "Benjamin Bonney, you're under arrest."

Bonney whipped his head around, struggling to get free from Hodgins' claw-like grasp. The detective grabbed Bonney's wrist with his free hand and twisted his arm behind his back, shoving him against the wall. A small Colt House Revolver tumbled from Bonney's suit jacket pocket.

Barnes hurried over and picked up the gun. Patrons gasped. A woman screamed. Another fainted, falling sideways out of her chair. Fortunately, her husband caught her before she hit the floor.

"Please, everyone stay in your seats. You're in no danger. Barnes, your cuffs."

Hodgins took the struggling criminal out, the man swearing all the way, while Barnes picked up Bonney's satchel and escorted Mrs. Bowdre like a lady, her hand resting on his forearm.

As they exited the dining room, the maître d' looked down his nose at Hodgins, a scowl on his face. The detective nodded and smiled. "As I said, discrete." He chuckled when the maître d' mumbled something Hodgins figured was less than complimentary.

Hodgins called out to a passing carriage to stop. Once Bonney was settled, Barnes assisted Mrs. Bowdre inside. She sat opposite her brother, glaring at him the entire way. Neither said a word. When they arrived at the police station, Barnes took Bonney inside while Hodgins paid the driver before helping Mrs. Bowdre down. Bonney was taken to a cell, but Hodgins took the sister into his office.

"Haven't decided yet if you belong in a cell or not. Tell me, why were you in the Queen's with your brother to wait for the train? Escaping across the border with ill-gotten goods?"

"No. My cad of a brother threatened me with that gun you found. He seemed confident no one would be looking for him, so agreed to wait at the hotel. My family has a reputation in New York, and I've tried to stay clear of it. Moving here with my husband was my chance to be free. Unfortunately, Benjamin wasn't satisfied with staying in New York, robbing whoever he could. I don't know how he became involved with the smuggling, but he managed to talk my husband into joining him. You have to believe me. I had no idea he'd kept the gems in my home."

Hodgins studied her expression and demeanour, trying to decide if she spoke the truth. "I believed you before, and I still do. You won't be punished for your husband's actions. However, I'm not convinced you aren't in it with your brother. Not yet, anyway. I need to speak with him. Stay here until I return."

The detective exited, closed his office door, and went to Riddell's desk. "Keep an eye on the lady, would you? Make certain she doesn't leave."

He made his way to the basement where Benjamin Bonney had been put, two cells past Bowdre. Barnes stood at a nearby table, going through something. "What have you, Henry?"

"Found all this when we searched the satchel." A cloth pouch, emptied of its contents, sat on the small table. Barnes stood aside.

"Is that what I think it is?" Hodgins picked up the ten-carat diamond, ignoring the smaller rubies, emeralds, and diamonds scattered around it.

"Looks like this may be the rest of the missing jewels. I need to compare it to the list the jeweller's provided, but it seems to be everything. I'm sure Mr. Fitzsimmons will be happy we found that diamond before it was sold."

"You check the list while I have a little chat with our guest." Hodgins left the jewels and stood in front of Bonney's cell. "You've been busy, Mr. Bonney. I assume Mr. Bowdre is part of this South Shore Goons gang I've been hearing about. What I don't know is which of you killed Dekker and Jorginsen. Or did you both participate?"

"Don't know what yer talking 'bout. Ain't killed no one. Just having a spot of lunch with my sister. Last I heard, it weren't against the law." Bonney leaned back against the wall behind the cot and examined his fingernails, paying little attention to the detective.

"A spot of lunch? With the sister you took at gunpoint? That's called kidnapping, and it *is* against the law."

Bonney shrugged. "That's your opinion."

Frustrated, Hodgins blew out a breath and unlocked Bowdre's cell door. "Come with me." He escorted Bowdre up to the interrogation room.

David Bowdre glanced back at Bonney, who ran his index finger across his throat. Beads of sweat formed on Bowdre's forehead.

The detective had a constable fetch a pad of foolscap and pencil and bring them to him. Once delivered, the constable was instructed to wait outside the door.

"Mr. Bowdre, has anyone informed you about your wife?"

Bowdre's eyes widened. "My wife? Has something happened? Is she all right?"

"Yes, she's fine. A little shaken up, though. Her loving brother took her at gunpoint after retrieving the rest of the stolen gems stashed in your home, intending to take the train back to New York."

"What? Why? How could he do such a thing to his sister? I need to see her."

"She's in my office. If you cooperate, I may let you speak to her. First, tell me why you stole the gems. You have steady employment and decent wages. Even own your house. What made you turn to robbery?"

Bowdre slumped. "I need to return to New York sooner than planned. I received a letter last month saying that both my parents are quite ill. I haven't saved enough money to move yet. They need expensive medical care." He paused and blew out a breath.

"When Benjamin showed up at my home, I thought him to be the miracle I prayed for. Steal a few gems, that's all. No one was meant to get hurt. He'd heard about the large ten-carat diamond and was contacted by someone out of the country willing to pay handsomely for it. He never told me who. The earlier robberies were not part of the original plan. The two Dutchmen were sent over to make sure the diamond was delivered, as promised."

Two, not three. Not Van Dijk. "But why did you kill them? Don't tell me it was an accident or self-defence. Both of them were stabbed multiple times, making it seem personal."

"Me? Kill them? No. It was all Bonney."

Hodgins picked up the pencil and tapped the table. "Can you prove that? Your brother-in-law hid the gems at your home, tying you to them. It follows that you murdered the Dutchmen to keep the jewels for yourself." Hodgins paused. "I wonder. I have an acquaintance in the New York Police, and he's provided information on Bonney. If I were to send another telegram inquiring about you, what would he find?"

"I… but… That was years ago. I was a young lad. He forced me to join him again."

"The stab wounds were made by two different blades. I think both you and Bonney stabbed the men. Unfortunately, I have no way to tie him to either the robberies or murders. Unless you tell me everything, the only crime he can be charged with is kidnapping. You'll stand trial for the thefts and murders. You alone will be held responsible. Are you willing to tell me every last detail? Provide some proof of his involvement?"

"Most of the stab wounds were done by Bonney. He even held his bloody knife to my throat, making me draw my knife across Dekker's neck. You do believe my wife is innocent? She knew nothing about her brother involving me or why. She can't be charged."

"It appears to me that she is simply a victim. No charges will be brought against her, but you must provide me with as much information as possible. Can you do that?"

"Yes."

Hodgins slid the pencil and foolscap across the table. "Write down everything from when he first contacted you up to your arrest."

Bowdre picked up the pencil and began writing. Hodgins sat watching for three-quarters of an hour until he finished, then had the constable take him back to the cells. "Keep him as far from Bonney as possible."

The constable nodded and led Bowdre away. Hodgins headed back to his office to chat with Mrs. Bowdre.

She sat back straight, facing his desk. An empty teacup rested on the edge of his desk in front of her.

"Would you like more tea?"

"No, thank you. My husband. Where is he?"

"In the cells. He's written out a full account of his involvement in the robberies and murders." Hodgins held up three pages full of Bowdre's writing.

She gasped. "Murder? No, not David."

"He's admitted as much, I'm afraid. He'll not get out of prison, and may hang. It's likely he'll be held responsible for it all, unless we can provide more than his word your brother was involved. As it stands, we can only charge your brother with kidnapping. You will provide a statement, won't you?"

She nodded. "He's my brother, and I don't want to see him in jail, but taking me at gunpoint is something I can *not* forgive. But what will become of me? I can't stay in Toronto on my own, and I can't go back to New York. The rest of my family won't take kindly to me being responsible for Benjamin being jailed." Her mouth formed a tiny circle as something came to her mind. "My brother won't be in jail forever, will he? He'll come after me."

Hodgins nodded, trying to think of a way to protect her from her criminal relatives. "Are there any friends elsewhere you can stay with?"

"Yes. I have a few childhood friends who married and moved away. I can write and ask if they will allow me to stay temporarily."

"Good. Might I suggest under the circumstances you procure a divorce? Over the years, I've made the acquaintance of several lawyers. I can recommend one that will be discreet. If you sell your house, you'll not be penniless. You can tell your friends your husband has died."

"Yes, I can sell the house, but a divorce? What will people think?"

"No one need ever know. As I said, I know someone who will make certain it's done quickly and quietly. It will be recorded at the courthouse, but kept out of the newspapers. First, I need you to write down everything from when your brother took you until we found you in the hotel dining room." He tore a sheet off his pad of foolscap and handed it to her, along with a pencil.

Mrs. Bowdre wiped the tears from her eyes and picked up the pencil. While she wrote, the detective took a sheet from his little notebook and jotted down the information for her.

When she finished, he handed the note to her. "The name and address of that lawyer, along with the estate agent I used when purchasing my house. He'll make certain you get a fair price. I suggest you start soon, today if possible."

"Thank you. Would you mind accompanying me to the lawyer's? I don't know what to do, and it is rather embarrassing."

"Of course. We can go now if you'd like. If he's not available, you can make an appointment. Excuse me a moment while I instruct my constables to gather as many statements as possible from contacts at the docks. Hopefully, we can also get your brother for the robberies and recruiting gang members, then shut down the gang permanently."

Five minutes later, the detective and Mrs. Bowdre made their way to the lawyer's to begin her new life.

CHAPTER TWENTY-SEVEN

week passed before Bowdre stood before the judge. He'd pled guilty and provided much-needed information, so the judge sentenced him to life in prison, sparing him from the noose.

The following week, Bonney would be on trial for kidnapping, robbery, and murder. He'd pled not guilty. With a written statement from his sister, the kidnapping charge would hold, but there was no proof he committed the murders. The sentence wouldn't be as long as Bowdre's, but would provide plenty of time for his sister to hide.

Barnes and Harrington obtained a few statements from dock workers, stating that Bonney tried to recruit them into his newly formed gang, the South Side Goons, to help rob the jewellery stores. None of the men actually recruited would speak to the police. He'd be behind bars twenty years for kidnapping, with an additional ten years for the three robberies.

With the cases finally closed, Hodgins took a much-needed day off. He slept in almost until noon for the first time in months, then enjoyed a leisurely breakfast with his wife. With the children playing in the backyard, Cordelia took the opportunity to ask about Mrs. Bowdry.

"I can't imagine the terror and heartache of being abducted by her own brother. Is she still in the city?"

"Yes, but not for much longer. None of her friends are aware she's obtained a divorce. It was official a few days ago. She still needs to sell the house, but she's already started telling people, like the estate agent, that she's a widow."

Cordelia blew on her hot tea, trying to cool it. "Where will she go? Certainly not back to her family in New York."

"No. She has an old friend in Texas. Husband's in oil. Mrs. Bowdre is a fine-looking woman, and although not wealthy, she'll have more than a few dollars to her name once the house is sold. I expect her friend will try to fix her up with a new husband when the proper mourning period is over. Delia, do you think she'll eventually tell her friend the truth about her ex-husband?"

"Not likely. Divorce is such a stigma for a woman. Add a criminal husband into it, and all except the closest of friends will abandon her, if she's lucky enough to have friends that close and understanding. She'd stand no chance at marrying again. She's better off sticking to the story of being widowed."

"Well, I wish her luck. She deserves to have a good life. Now, are there any scrambled eggs left? I'm famished."

Reviews are Golden

I would love to hear from you! Please consider leaving a review on your favourite social media platform, Amazon, or Goodreads.

Reviews mean the world to authors. Not only do we enjoy reading how you felt about the book, but they help other readers get a feel for a book in advance, and aid authors in marketing.

If you wish to hear about the progress of any of my books, please join my newsletter at:
https://landing.mailerlite.com/webforms/landing/u0q5f2

Previous books can be found on Amazon at
https://www.amazon.com/stores/Nanci-M-Pattenden/author/B01L5L2TSS

Thank you for coming on this adventure with me.

ABOUT THE AUTHOR

Nanci M. Pattenden is a genealogist and an emerging fiction writer, currently working on a collection of detective stories set in Victorian Toronto and an Urban Fantasy trilogy, Generation Witch. She also co-authors a funny paranormal series, D.E.M.ON. Tales.

She has completed the Creative Writing program at both the University of Calgary and the University of Toronto.

Nanci currently resides in Newmarket with her adorable cat Freya.

nanci@nancipattenden.com
www.murderdoespayink.ca
www.nancipattenden.com
@npattenden